D1525500

PRAISE FOR LAWRENCE GROBEL

"Larry Grobel's writing is quite marvelous." — **J.P. Donleavy**

"I have come to know Larry Grobel very well. I have learned to appreciate his manner, his style, over the years. He has a genuine interest in people, which is why he's such a good writer."
— **Al Pacino**

"One can discern in Larry...a quality of personality that is fundamentally moral, without being moralistic."
— **Joyce Carol Oates**

"I would recommend Larry Grobel as a therapist to just about anybody." — **Montel Williams**

"Larry is profoundly entertaining...and extremely insane."
– **Diane Keaton**

"Lawrence Grobel has spent a lifetime becoming a great writer. And we are the beneficiaries. Read on and count your blessings!"
— **Noah benShea**, **author,** *Jacob the Baker* **series of books**

"I think I could read Lawrence Grobel forever. He deserves a chunk of your reading time; he's able to take you in directions you didn't think you'd be heading." — **Clay Smith,** *Austin Chronicle*

"A legend among journalists." — *Writer's Digest*

"Lawrence Grobel has been known for his award-winning journalism, but now he has turned his talents to fiction, and these stories demand attention."

— Will Manus, playwright, critic

"I've been doing my show for 17 years. Larry Grobel is the reason I'm here. His work is so profound."

— Elvis Mitchell, NPR's "The Treatment"

"Lawrence Grobel's stories are like a mirror that reveals our strengths, our weaknesses, and our games in an entertaining, eye-opening way." — **Rita Settimo,** *Michigan Advisor*

ACCLAIM FOR *THE NARCISSIST:* STORIES

"These stories showcase Grobel's versatility, ranging from Africa and India to Bangkok and Paris, from funeral parlors to cancer wards, from spoiled Beverly Hills teenagers to stand-up-comedy. He casts a wide net and doesn't once miss his mark."

— Adrienne Kennedy, Obie Award-winning playwright

"Some of these stories are haunting, others are wickedly humorous or sarcastic, but all are unforgettable. Grobel has shown a new, highly original side to himself as a writer and it's a side well worth your time." — **David Assael, screen and TV writer**

Lawrence Grobel

SCHEMERS, DREAMERS, CHEATERS, BELIEVERS

Lawrence Grobel is the author of 29 books. Among his honors are a National Endowment for the Arts Fellowship for his fiction; Special Achievement Awards from PEN for his *Conversations with Capote*, and *Playboy* for his interviews with Barbra Streisand, Marlon Brando and Al Pacino; and the Prix Litteraire from The Syndicat Francais de la Critique de Cinema for his *Al Pacino: In Conversation with Lawrence Grobel*. He has been a Contributing Editor for *Playboy, Movieline, World* (New Zealand), and *Trendy* (Poland). He served in the Peace Corps, teaching at the Ghana Institute of Journalism; created the M.F.A. in Professional Writing for Antioch University; and taught in the English and Honors Departments at UCLA. He has served as a jury member at the annual Camerimage Film Festival in Poland and has appeared as himself in the documentary *Salinger* and Al Pacino's docudrama *Wilde Salome*. His works have been translated into fourteen languages. *Schemers, Cheaters, Dreamers, Believers* is his second book of short stories, written between May and October 2020, during the Covid-19 pandemic.

Books by Lawrence Grobel

Fiction
Schemers, Cheaters, Dreamers, Believers
The Narcissist
Begin Again Finnegan
Catch a Fallen Star
The Black Eyes of Akbah
Commando Ex

Memoir
You Show Me Yours

Poetry
Madonna Paints a Mustache & Other Celebrity Happenings

Non-fiction
You, Talking to Me
Meryl Streep
Barbra Streisand
Conversations with Ava Gardner
Marilyn & Me (for Lawrence Schiller)
Signing In: 50 Celebrity Profiles
"I Want You in My Movie!" The Making of Al Pacino's Wilde Salome
Yoga? No! Shmoga!

Icons: 15 Celebrity Profiles
Al Pacino: In Conversation with Lawrence Grobel
Conversations with Robert Evans
The Art of the Interview: Lessons from a Master of the Craft
Climbing Higher (with Montel Williams)
Endangered Species: Writers Talk About Their Craft,
Their Vision, Their Lives
Above the Line: Conversations About the Movies
Conversations with Michener
The Hustons
Conversations with Brando
Conversations with Capote

Screenplays
Volume 1 (Conversations with Brando & The Black Eyes of Akbah)
Volume 2 (Catch a Fallen Star & Begin Again Finnegan)

www.lawrencegrobel.com

SCHEMERS, DREAMERS, CHEATERS, BELIEVERS

STORIES WRITTEN DURING THE 2020 PANDEMIC

LAWRENCE GROBEL

HMH Press
Copyright 2021 Lawrence Grobel
contact@lawrencegrobel.com
Cover Design: Paul Singer
Author Photo: Lawrence Grobel

ISBN: 9798561394430

for Maya & Hana,
who, one day, may find the time

"It was the best of times, it was the worst of times,
it was the age of wisdom, it was the age of foolishness,
it was the epoch of belief, it was the epoch of incredulity,
it was the season of Light, it was the season of Darkness,
it was the spring of hope, it was the winter of despair … …
we had nothing before us,
we were all going direct to Heaven,
we were all going the other way …."

— Charles Dickens, *A Tale of Two Cities*

"It's like a miracle—one day, it will disappear."

—President Donald Trump, Feb. 27, 2020

CONTENTS

SCHEMERS

MIRACLE

1

Me fatha he be angry with me if he know. That is why I wear long-long cloths, wrapped loose around me waist. If he sees me belly getting bigger, he beat me. He call me foolish girl. I am foolish girl. But I don't let him see me like this. Me fatha have a very bad temper.

That is why I stay with Mum. She be understanding. She tels me to have baby but leave it somewhere. She say that fourteen years is too young to be a mum, and she say she no can care for me and baby since we stay in one room and baby cry and keep us all up when should be sleeping. And she say we no can afford to have baby now. I know she right, and I know I must stay away from me fatha until this be done with.

Life be hard. I not suppose to be with child. It just happen. No one tell me the way it happens. The boy, no one tell him. I think sex something you do to enjoy. But I should have been told the different ways to do it, and that you can protect yourself from getting with child. Me mum say she forget how old I am and that I would be doing these things. She has a very hard life. Me fatha has not helped her and that makes it so hard.

I have find a place to have baby and leave it. It outside village, under small bridge over a river now dry. It make me sad *to leave baby there, but what else can I do? No one take it here and me mum say I too young to be responsible for it.*

It be God's will. Whatever happens, it be God's will.

2

When the baby was ready to come out, Akosua walked to the wooden bridge and sat in the shade beneath it, by a small boulder. Her mother had said she would come, but she had other children to care for and wasn't able to get there to help. So Akosua was alone when her water broke. She leaned against the boulder for support and pushed like she had been told by her mother. It hurt to push. When the pain increased, she squatted and pushed harder until she could feel the head. She cupped her hands under its head and pushed even harder. The baby slipped out from her body and into her hands. It was slimy like a fish. Her mother had given her a scissors to cut the umbilical cord, and told her that after she tied it, she should pull the cord out of her until it all came out.

This be me baby, Akosua thought. *But I dont look at it because I have to leave it.*

When some of her strength returned, she cut a piece of her cloth to wrap the baby, then gathered loose dirt into a small mound like a cradle and placed the baby on top. She drank some water from a plastic bottle and then walked slowly back to the village. The baby remained behind, on a dirt pile, in the shade under the bridge.

3

When Akosua reached the village the dog from a neighboring compound came running to her. "Hey, Cacao," she said, bending to pet the friendly brown mongrel named after a bean. The dog sniffed her crotch and Akosua shooed him away. She entered her small compound and saw her mother pounding cassava. They nodded to each other indicating the deed was done. It was not something either one wanted to talk about.

4

The next day, eight-year-old Kofi and his twin brother Ansah, came into Akosua's compound asking if she had seen their dog, Cacao. "Yesterday," Akosua told them. The boys were worried because the dog had been missing all night. They thanked Akosua for the news and went on to the other compounds, asking the villagers if they had seen Cacao. A few remembered seeing him running towards Akosua, but that was all. The boys decided to separate, calling Cacao's name on the north and south sides of the village.

They had no luck finding their dog that day, but the following day they walked outside the village, calling the dog's name. When they approached the old wooden bridge, Ansah said he thought he saw something. The boys approached, and there was Cacao, wagging his tail, happy to see them.

But the dog didn't stand up and didn't go to them when they called his name. "Look," Kofi said. He saw that Cacao was curled around a piece of cloth on top of a small dirt mound. Then they heard the baby's whimper.

5

The boys and the dog became immediate heroes in the village, and word soon spread to other villages and then to the city. A reporter from the national newspaper arrived to get the boys' story and to take photographs of them, of Cacao, and of the baby.

It was a miracle that the baby had survived. When the boys carried the infant to their compound, their mother, who was nursing her own baby, asked where they had found her. Then she offered the weakened baby her breast and brought her back to life. "Look how she suckles," the woman laughed. "Like a pig."

The village chief came to see the baby and then called for a council meeting. Someone had left the baby to die, and they wanted to know who it was. All the villagers were asked about it, but no one confessed. Akosua and her mother said nothing.

The council concluded it was a mystery and that the infant probably had come from another village. The reporter who showed up couldn't solve the mystery, but he shrewdly focused his story on the dog. Everyone in the village agreed that it was Cacao who saved the baby by staying with her, providing the warmth she needed to make it through the nights. Strangers came to the village to see the dog, and many offered to buy him.

No one offered to take the baby.

6

But then the story reached distant shores, and suddenly there was great interest in adopting the child. Families from Europe, and North and South America got in touch with the newspaper inquiring about her. They were given the email address and phone number of the local commissioner in charge of the area where the baby was found. His name was Mr. Joseph Owusu.

The commissioner quickly understood the situation. These foreign families were not all offering to take the baby only out of the goodness of their hearts; many were desperate to have a child and were willing to pay anything to get one. Mr. Owusu explained to all those who reached out to him that he couldn't be sure about the legalities of allowing a foreigner to adopt an abandoned child, but he would put their names on a list and do everything he could to help them. There would be some expenses, he told them, and anything they might contribute would go a long way to a successful conclusion. He noted that there were many people contacting him and those who paid a little more would demonstrate that they could better provide for the child than those who paid less. Within a month, Mr. Owusu was able to deposit over $50,000 into his bank account. And he came to this conclusion: If so many foreigners wanted this infant, the only true solution would be to keep the child himself.

He named her Miracle.

7
16 Years Later

Chuck Brown was twenty-one when he graduated from the University of Michigan and joined the Peace Corps. He was assigned to a country in West Africa that he knew nothing about, and as part of his in-country training, he was sent to a northern village to live with a family while learning the language and teaching for a month at a middle school. The family that took him in was more like an orphanage for stray children, led by a former commissioner who had a drinking problem. His name was Mr. Joseph Owusu.

There were ten children ranging in ages from four to sixteen at this compound and all of them took a liking to the fair-haired Chuck. They would gather around after dinner and listen to him read them stories while they stroked the hair on his arms and legs and combed his straight hair. At first, Chuck felt like a pet or a zoo animal, but after a while he looked forward to the time he spent with these children. Mr. Owusu, however, was another matter.

"Come and drink with me," Mr. Owusu would say after the children were all in bed.

Chuck would join Mr. Owusu at the local bar and listen to him tell how he once made a lot of money off the oldest child under his care. "She was abandoned as a baby," he explained. "A dog found her under a bridge and stayed with her for two days, keeping her warm and alive. Everybody in the country made a big deal about the dog and people all over the world got in touch with me because they wanted to adopt the baby. I was the commissioner at the time, so I was in charge. Some people sent me ten thousand dollars to get that child. In the end, I decided it would be best if I took her in myself. Named her Miracle."

Chuck didn't say anything while Mr. Owusu talked, but he narrowed his eyes as he looked at him. Owusu was a lousy drunk, he thought. There was no sense telling him that when he was five, his family had offered to adopt that baby. He had heard his father tell the story over the years, how he had sent this man three-thousand dollars to deal with the paperwork, only to find out later that dozens of other families had also been fleeced by this crooked man. Chuck's parents had often wondered aloud what had happened to that child, and how different her life might have been had they been able to raise her.

And then Mr. Owusu said something astounding to Chuck Brown.

"You have become part of our family," he said. "And when you leave next week, I would like you to leave behind something, so that we will always remember you, and you will never forget us. Miracle is now sixteen," he went on. "She's of an age to bear children. I would like you to be the father of her first child."

"Do you consider me your son?" Chuck said, remembering how often Mr. Owusu introduced Chuck to the other villagers as his new son from the States.

"Yes, for the time you are here, you are my son."

"That would make Miracle my sister then," Chuck said.

"Nonsense," Mr. Owusu said. "She's an orphan."

"But you took her in. You kept her from growing up with a loving family in another country, from getting a good education, going to college, from being someone she may never get to be."

"It was too hard to choose," Mr. Owusu said. "And too much paperwork and palaver. Do you know how many palms I'd have had to dash to get her a passport when she didn't have a family name, and no one knew where she came from? And what would they have done with such a girl, from no family? An orphan; saved by a dog. She was bad luck."

"Could it have been done?" Chuck asked.

"With enough money, yes, I suppose."

"And you certainly had enough money from all those families."

"That money paid for my compound. And for my car. We have to look after ourselves before we look after others."

"Just seems a shame that Miracle got caught by your greed. Sounds like she was good luck for you."

"You are talking nonsense, and you are insulting me. Getting back to what Miracle needs now — you can give her a child."

"I prefer not to," Chuck said.

"Just think about it. You're here for one more week. It only takes one fuck."

8

Chuck's letter to his parents began, "Are you ready to hear a miracle?" He wrote a detailed description of his time in the village and of Mr. Joseph Owusu's drunken proposition. And he concluded by asking them if they'd still like to perform a true miracle by bringing Miracle to the States, enrolling her in the high school where he went to school, and making her, all these years later, a true part of their family.

He didn't know how they would respond, but he liked to think that miracles do happen.

GIN

When the Covid-19 pandemic hit and people were told to stay home, Lee and Olivia Stein made a pact with the devil. They would play two card games every day—Casino and Gin Rummy—and keep score. The Casino win would be worth 25 points. If one of them got all eleven points, it would be worth an extra 25 points. Each gin game would be worth ten points plus whatever the amount of the cards the loser got stuck with, minus those they could lay off. They could play as many games as they chose each day and the first person to reach ten thousand points, or who was ahead when a vaccine was found and/or the pandemic was declared over, would get to choose whether to kill or be killed by the other.

Lee was 82 and Olivia 80 when they started playing. Both of them suffered from memory loss, painful arthritis, aching bones, pre-diabetes, heart palpitations, soft teeth that occasionally cracked, muscle cramps, glaucoma, and ever-rising blood pressure due to a deep hatred of the mean and disgraceful Republicans who had no empathy for the downtrodden, the trodden, or anyone who wasn't an American Firster. They were ready to kiss the world goodbye before the pandemic. Instead, they decided to make a game of it.

The devil? Well, it had to be the devil in each of them that got them to make such a pact. Or maybe it was the godawful president, whom some (including Lee and Olivia) considered the Anti-Christ. But that is neither here nor there. Their pact was made, the games were played, and the score was meticulously kept.

Lee did most of the commentary when they played, sometimes mentally focusing on a card he needed and when Olivia threw it down, he would exclaim, "Ha! I knew it. I've got psychic powers. I kept thinking, 'Throw the four of clubs, the four of clubs.' And you did! And that, my dear, is gin."

When Olivia won, she simply turned her last throwing card over and asked, "How much?"

Lee got to a thousand first, a hundred and forty points ahead of Olivia, which made him gloat, "Only nine thousand to go." When he blanked her in a Casino game, earning an extra 25 points, he couldn't keep from analyzing the mistakes she made that would have at least gotten her the deuce of spades. She tolerated his obnoxious remarks up to a point, but when he started humming "Just like a woman," she would tell him that even Bob Dylan had a better voice than he did.

"You love Dylan as much as I do," Lee would say. "Even if you think 'Mr. Tambourine Man' and 'Like a Rolling Stone,' are better than 'Not Dark Yet' and 'Knockin' on Heaven's Door.'"

"You just relate more to his death songs. You can't wait to have them played at your funeral."

"That shows you how little you know," Lee would say. "I want 'Idiot Wind,' and 'Romance in Durango.'" Then Lee would sing the four lines he remembered, "*Hot chili peppers in the blistering sun…., Me and Magdalena on the run…, Soon the horse will take us to Durango…, Soon you will be dancing the fandango …*"

Dylan was a constant in their lives. They listened to him whenever they used to take car trips, they had given him the most songs in their iPod Shuffles, and they had opened the bottle of wine they were saving for a special occasion on the day he won the Nobel Prize. His songs gave them endless hours of comparisons to the Boss, the Beatles, Paul Simon, and Joan Baez. But it wasn't just Dylan vs. others; they often took sides comparing Mozart and Chopin, Picasso and Matisse, Philip Roth and Saul Bellow, Chris Burden and Paul McCarthy. They liked to think how much better the world would have been had John Lennon, Eva Cassady, and Jim Morrison lived to old age.

Arguing about any of this was pleasurable, as compared to when it came to the current state of politics, and the politicization of the pandemic. The state of the world brought them down, made them angry, and yet they couldn't keep from watching Chris Hayes, Rachel Maddow, and Lawrence O'Donnell on MSNBC. At least those three were speaking for them. But when Lee turned to Fox to shout back at the Wish-I-Could-Punch-Him-in-the-Face Sean Hannity or the I-Want-to-Strangle Laura Ingraham, Olivia went to another room to watch something—anything—else.

When Lee reached two thousand points to Olivia's sixteen hundred, he complained of a crick in his elbow. "You think it's cancer?" he wondered.

"Everything's cancer with you," Olivia said. "Your toe aches, it's cancer. The mole on your hand is cancer. A headache is a tumor. A spider bite is a lump. You should have been dead thirty years ago."

"And you?" Lee responded. "Because you don't complain you don't think I know what you're thinking? You worry plenty. I just speak for the two of us."

"Speak for yourself, leave me out of your cancers."

"You do realize," Lee said, "that there's not going to be a cure for this Covid in our lifetime. They'll find a vaccine, but it's not going to eradicate it."

"You don't think I know that?"

"So, the cards are really our endgame."

"That's right—it's our Final Solution. At least for one of us."

"You'd better start winning," Lee said, "Or it'll soon be over for you, Baby Blue."

"Just because you're ahead now, don't get cocky. We've still got a ways to go."

Olivia caught up with Lee at their halfway mark, both of them reaching five thousand points the same week. But luck was with Lee for the next few thousand points and by the time of the 2020 election, it looked like he had an insurmountable lead. He wondered to himself whether they should slow down the pace of their games. The thought crossed both of their minds that if they stopped playing before either reached ten thousand, there would be no winner who got to choose who lived and who died. Then again, they also both thought of doubling their pace, just for one of them, at least, to get it over with.

When Lee scored his nine thousandth point, Olivia accused him of looking at her cards. "I know you do that," she said. "I see the way you sideways glance."

"Why would I cheat when I beat you straight up? I'm just the better player. And I can read you. You have a lot of tells."

"You're just lucky, there's no skill in Casino. It's just the cards you're dealt."

"I don't agree," Lee said. "You say that because you don't realize how much skill there is. Gin for sure. But even Casino."

"You don't even keep a fair score. How many times have you figured or recorded my score wrong?"

"When I make a mistake, you catch it. You're always catching, because you don't trust me."

"How can I trust you if you make mistakes? You never make a mistake with your score, unless you add up, not down."

"You think I do this on purpose? Then why don't you keep the score. I don't care."

"Maybe I should," Olivia said.

"Okay, do."

"I don't want to."

"I know you don't. Just admit it, you're not a good card player."

"And you are?"

"Who's winning?"

"You know something?" Olivia asked, disgusted, "Why don't we call it now? You win. Okay? You want me to kill you, I'll do it."

"Is that what you think will happen when I win? Maybe I'll kill you."

"Fine, do it."

"I will," Lee said.

"I wish you would," Olivia said.

"You think I won't?"

"I think the only way I'm going to die is if I commit suicide. Because you don't have it in you," Olivia said. "I always knew I'd have to choose killing you if I won, because that's the only way you'll be put out of our misery."

"Misery is right," Lee said. "You're miserable to live with."

"And you're no picnic, always complaining about your aches and pains. You think your aches are worse than mine?"

"Yes, I do."

"That's because you don't know how I really feel. I don't cry over every step."

"And I do?"

"Yes, you do."

"So why don't you shoot me?" Lee asked.

"Who said anything about shooting? We don't even own a gun. I'll kill you with poison."

"And I'll kill you with a pillow."

But neither killed the other that day. In fact, Lee started to lose most of their next few weeks' games on purpose, to allow Olivia to catch up. But Olivia caught him throwing away a winning hand and got furious with him. "You think you can let me win and get away with it? I quit. I'm just going to kill myself. I don't need you."

"You can't quit. We made a pact," Lee said.

"And you violated it."

"No, I didn't. We never said how we would strategize. If I get pleasure out of squeezing you like a Panic Pete toy, that's just my game. You don't even have a game."

"You think you're so smart? Well, maybe you should start sleeping with one eye open."

"And maybe you should stop talking."

"You're the one who's always talking," Olivia said.

"All right, enough. Shuffle and deal already."

THE GATHERING

Parnell Jones lived in his house on the slope of a fashionable canyon for twenty-five years and never had a problem with any of his neighbors until the house that bordered his backyard was sold and the new owner refused to trim or prune his trees and bushes on the edge of his property. There was a chain link fence as well, but that long ago was covered by ivy.

The problem with Glenn, his new neighbor, began when Parnell asked him to trim some of the pine and eucalyptus trees that showered both yards with their needles and leaves. Glenn said the trees' shedding made good compost for their lawns. Parnell complained that the pine needles blanketed his lawn and clogged the drains. He had to rake them into piles twice a week for three of the four seasons. But Glenn refused to do anything about it. When Parnell offered to split the cost of trimming the tallest pine, the one that blocked the sun for most of the day, his neighbor said he liked the way the mighty tree looked. When Parnell sought permission for a tree arborist to enter Glenn's yard to climb into the pine and cut only the branches and leaves overhanging on his side, he was denied. When Parnell threatened a lawsuit, his neighbor, a lawyer, shrugged and said, "Knock yourself out." So, Parnell stewed, and learned to live with the tree as it continued to grow, casting its shadow across his yard and onto his roof.

It wasn't just that the tree blocked the sun and shed its needles all over Parnell's yard and gutters; it also caused him anxiety during the storm seasons because if it ever fell, it would reach his house and do considerable damage. Added to that, the tree attracted squirrels, rats, insects and birds of all kinds. It was so big, there was ample room for hawks and nuthatches, owls and mockingbirds, bluebirds and chickadees, and dozens of other species. When they chirped, squawked, or hummed it made it difficult for Parnell to read a book or newspaper outside. What he often did instead was clean and polish his Beeman QB Chief air rifle and his H&R pump shotgun, fantasizing the ways in which he might accidentally shoot his neighbor and get away with it.

Parnell was a strong advocate of the good-fences-make-good-neighbors philosophy, but even if Parnell put up a twenty-foot wall between them, the pine tree would still hover over it like a goliath. Fences be damned! Glenn just wasn't a good neighbor.

One summer morning, Parnell saw a squirrel gnawing on the electrical wire that connected from a pole in the street to his roof. The wire crossed over Glenn's property as well. Parnell grabbed his pellet rifle and took aim, knocking the squirrel off the wire and into Glenn's yard. The "bushy-tailed rat," as Parnell liked to call the varmints, had been shot in the eye. It bled and squeaked as Glenn came out to see what had happened. It led to a heated exchange of words between the neighbors, ending with Glenn saying now he'd *never* trim any of his trees, because they serve to protect wildlife from the likes of Parnell.

The following week, there were more birds in those trees than ever before. So many of them sent their droppings onto Parnell's flower beds and roof that you couldn't tell a carnation from a chrysanthemum. Parnell chose birdshot over pellets, the shotgun over the air rifle, and dispatched hundreds of birds and squirrels from the tall pine. A junco, a sparrow, and a nutcracker fell dead onto his neighbor's property.

Glenn called the police.

Disputes between neighbors can escalate quickly and get ugly, but often the police are torn between whose rights have been violated. In this instance, Parnell had to show his gun license and he took the cops on a tour of his backyard and roof, still covered in white bird shit. "What am I supposed to do?" he complained. "He won't trim his trees, I've lost any sun I used to have, it smells terrible, and I'm having to clean and rake every fucking day. I've tried to be reasonable, but the guy's an asshole, if you'll pardon my French."

The cops knew Parnell. He wasn't a troublemaker. They didn't want to fine him. They said they'd let him off with a warning this time, and suggested if he must target practice, stick with the air rifle.

But then the crows came. Large black blots against the blue sky. They came in murders of five, ten, twenty, as if coming to a Comic-Con convention or a political rally. They filled the branches of the tall pine and the nearby eucalyptus. They seemed to have a purpose, to have things to discuss, like sharing newly discovered ways to open a jar's lid or maneuver around a live electrical wire. Their excrement left much larger markings on Parnell's plants, grass and patio. Their cawing was ugly and ominous. Some of them were larger than the others and Parnell figured they must be ravens. He knew that his pellet rifle wouldn't scare off these big birds. So, he loaded the H&R with birdshot shells, said to hell with the warning, and squeezed the trigger.

But the black birds were not swallows or sapsuckers or woodpeckers. They weren't going to fly away from a fight. These were among the most intelligent species of birds and when they saw one of their own drop from the birdshot, they began to squawk and caw in unison, and before long there were twice as many of them and they just kept coming. Parnell stood on his patio, shotgun at his side, marveling at how quickly the sky had turned dark with crows.

But he didn't stand there for long. When the birds started circling overhead, he backed up against the sliding glass door. When one of the biggest, darkest crows, with a four-foot wingspan and a beak as thick as a baseball bat handle and as deadly as a samurai sword, flapped his broad wings rapidly, and dive-bombed straight in his direction, he panicked and quickly reached his hand behind, slid the door open and ducked inside the safety of his house, just as the large crow hit the thick glass, beak and head first.

The impact was so fierce that the glass cracked but didn't shatter. The crow fell to the ground, a yellow pus oozing from his eyes and mouth. He let out a yelp, a sound of pain and anger familiar to crows. The gathering in the sky and on the branches of the backyard pines and eucalyptuses dialed up their squawking, sounding their alarm. Their leader had fallen.

And then began the incessant crowing. The screaming. The sky further blackened as more and more crows and conspiracies of ravens began to arrive. The branches grew heavy under the weight of so many large birds. It had begun with twenty or thirty of them, but had multiplied into the hundreds, circling Parnell's house, divebombing into his windows.

Crows and ravens were exceptional birds, but their blackness separated them from all the colorful, beloved, pretty birds that each of the fifty states in the U.S. chose as their state bird. Fifty different birds representing fifty states, yet none of them the crow, raven or grackle, because they were the birds of mythological, demonic power. The flying metaphors of death and destruction.

And here they gathered, to seek revenge against the man who caused the death of their leader.

Parnell had had his share of bar fights and sports brawls, but the odds of defeating or outsmarting these crows were not in his favor. The birds so greatly outnumbered him that he knew it would be useless to try and pick them off a few at a time with his shotgun. He kept a box of rat poison under the kitchen sink and tried soaking the poison in bread which he threw onto his lawn. The bread was eaten by some rats and squirrels, but not the crows. What he didn't know was that Glenn was feeding them dog food pellets, old fruit, and peanuts in the shell, encouraging the birds to stick around to continue their harassment of Parnell.

In the middle of the night, Parnell would sneak outside to hang cording with reflective CDs throughout his yard, along with bird tape streamers. He climbed onto his roof and placed bird spikes and ceramic owls. He tried an ultrasonic bird repeller. He blasted loud heavy metal music through speakers he put by the backyard windows. But what he learned about these dark birds was that when they were angry, they lost any fear and ignored any discomfort. Nothing Parnell tried could stop them.

When he pulled his car out of the garage, the crows covered the windshield with their excrement. They sat on the car's roof, pecking into the soft aluminum. They flew along each side of the car until it became impossible for him to continue driving.

Forced to stay inside his house, his windows cracked, his backyard ruined, his roof beginning to collapse under the weight of massive bird shit and hundreds of resting crows, Parnell called his neighbor Glenn and pleaded with him to chop down his trees, offering to pay whatever the cost to get it done.

"I've got a proposition for you," Glenn countered.

"If it gets rid of these birds, I'll do it."

"Sell me your house," Glenn said.

"What?"

"I'm not touching my trees. And the birds aren't bothering me. They're after you, Parnell. Whatever you did to stir their rancor, you succeeded. They're not going away, and they're driving you crazy. Literally. So, sell me your house and find another one to live in."

"You've got that kind of money?" Parnell asked. "This house is worth at least two million."

"Not anymore," Glenn said. "The way it is now, it's unsellable. I will give you five-hundred thousand dollars, and I'll take it as is."

"You're out of your mind," Parnell said.

"That's a matter of perspective. From where I'm sitting, I think the shoe's on the other foot."

"I'd rather live with the crows than sell you my house," Parnell barked.

"And I'll keep feeding them, to make sure you do," Glenn said.

Two days later, buckshot was fired from Parnell's house through the giant pine, shattering a few of Glenn's windows. The crows grew even more agitated than before and sullied the sky over Parnell's house. Parnell kept shooting at his neighbor's house until the police arrived. This time, they had no choice.

The crows flew in four columns like an overhead procession, accompanying the police car with Parnell handcuffed inside as it drove to the station. To keep Glenn from pressing charges, he agreed to sell him his house for half what Glenn had offered.

The crows were glad to be rid of him.

WHEN SHE WAS TWELVE

For her twelfth birthday, Mary's mother gave her a choice: a party or a present. Mary remembered her last birthday party where she received a dozen presents from her friends and wondered why her mother was making this offer.

"A party means food, party favors, cleaning before and after. I just thought that if you had something special you would like, I'd be happy to get it for you in lieu of a party. Either way, your choice."

"I'd like a digital tape recorder," Mary said. "A Sony UX560. It cost a hundred dollars."

"How do you know this?" her mother asked.

"I've been saving for it. It has a lot of good reviews."

"I had no idea you wanted a tape recorder," her mother said. "How come?"

"To record things," Mary said.

"What kind of things?" her mother wondered.

"Oh, you know. Birds. My friends. My voice when I sing. That kind of stuff."

What Mary really wanted to record were some of the crazy fights her parents had. Her father could be very threatening when he got angry, and she worried that he might one day go beyond yelling and hit her mother.

"All right," her mother said. "That'll be your present this year."

Twelve is a seminal year for a young girl. Not yet a teenager. Her body is developing. Her thoughts are turning towards things she might do but not tell her mother. If she's a serious girl, she will start discovering books and art that may influence her. She's beginning to see the world and her relationship to it differently. If she's immature, she'll be running with her friends, sharing likes and dislikes, bands that play music that moves her, dance steps that will make her giggle, training bras that will make the best use of what she's beginning to have. It's also a difficult year if your parents don't get along. You're too young to run away and live on your own, but old enough to understand what's going on. There were days when Mary wished she was a blissfully ignorant five-year-old, and other days when she wished she was seventeen and ready to leave home for college. Twelve was still a long way from seventeen, and an even longer way from the innocence of five.

Her father was always under a lot of stress. He wasn't his own boss and resented having to please those above him whom he didn't respect. He left home early and returned late. When his wife complained about her day, whatever that entailed, he didn't want to hear about it. He just wanted to come home to a prepared dinner, drink a beer, and watch TV. When his daughter wanted to show him what she had done in school or ask for his help with her homework, he didn't want to be bothered. He wanted to be left alone.

But when you live in a house with others, you can't really be left alone. And when those others are your family, you have an obligation to relate to them, to listen to what they've been thinking, and to share their hopes and dreams as they expect you to do the same. But Mary's father wanted none of that.

"Daddy," Mary said. "Can I go to a concert with my friends?"

"No, you're too young."

"No, I'm not. All my friends are going."

"No, it's too expensive."

"How do you know?"

"What did I just say?"

"You said …"

"Don't get smart with me, girl. Now, leave me alone."

This played out differently when it was his wife who asked for something.

"We need a new dishwasher," she'd say.

"What's wrong with the one we got?"

"It's not cleaning the dishes."

"So, use the sink."

"The dryer is not drying our clothes."

"Do you know how much those repairmen charge? Air dry them."

"What's wrong with you? The roof needs fixing, the bathroom faucet drips, the carpets are worn out and they smell. If we don't take care of things, they'll only get worse."

And then their fight would begin. He would yell at her; she would yell back. He would throw down the newspaper or the *TV Guide* and threaten her; she would stand her ground. He would make a fist; she would clench her jaw.

Mary would hide in her room, trying not to hear them. But they were loud, and they sometimes threw things, and her mother would often cry. Many of the curse words they exchanged were new to Mary when she first heard them, but were part of her vocabulary by the time she was twelve

Once Mary got her birthday present, she began to record these ugly transactions between them. Her hope was that one day, when the time was right, she would sit down with them and play what she recorded. If they heard what she heard, maybe it would stop. Especially if they realized that their behavior was all Mary knew about what marriage was.

But things don't usually work out to favor a child trying to teach her parents a lesson. Up until Mary hit "Play" on her Sony UX560, Mary had been spared physical abuse. Like her mother, she was the recipient of a lot of verbal abuse from her father; unlike her mother, she had never felt the back of his hand, or the spray of saliva from his mouth three inches from her face.

That changed three months after her twelfth birthday. As did her life.

When Mary played back her parents' latest fight, her father grabbed the tape recorder and threw it. He meant to throw it against the wall, hoping to break it, but it hit the top of the La-Z-Boy and landed, intact, on the seat. Mary rushed to get it and then ran to her room.

"You tape any more of us, that machine is trash," her father yelled, letting loose a series of threats aimed at intimidating her, as if that was necessary.

From behind her door, Mary recorded his tirade.

Then she heard her mother start screaming at him and recorded that.

Her father shouted that he was the boss in the family and his daughter would listen to him or regret it. Her mother shouted that Mary had every right to live her life free of fear and being bullied by him. The next sound Mary recorded was her mother tumbling into the table where the lamp was, and the crash of the lamp to the floor. "You sonofabitch!" her mother yelled. Mary heard her mother's footsteps, and then her father's, as he chased her into the kitchen.

She opened her door, holding the small recorder in her palm, and followed behind them. She saw her mother waving a carving knife, threating her husband that if he came any closer, she would use it. She screamed, "I'm warning you; I'm going to kill you!"

He rushed her.

She stabbed him in his chest.

He fell to the floor. "You bitch! You fucking bitch!"

"Go to hell," her mother yelled. "Die, you coward! You deserve it."

Mary, shocked and bewildered, dropped the recorder and stood frozen at the bloody tableau before her. How had it led to this? What should she do?

When her mother regained her senses, she saw Mary standing there and told her to call 911. "Tell them we need an ambulance."

But it was too late for her father, who died on the way to the hospital. And when the police interrogated both mother and daughter, it sounded like a family dispute that ended in self-defense. Right up until they found Mary's tape recorder on the floor where she dropped it and pressed *Rewind*.

The trial made the news and just a few months after the incident, Mary's mother was sentenced to ten years in prison. Mary was sent to live with her father's older brother and ditzy aunt in Florida.

She never liked her aunt and uncle, but being twelve, she had no say in the matter. They agreed to take her and that was that. But they didn't take to her.

"You're like your mother," her uncle would say whenever she said or did something they didn't like.

"She killed your brother," her aunt would chime in. "Look at her, doesn't look like him at all. Look at those little titties on her."

"Call them tits?" her uncle would say. "Show her what tits're supposed to look like."

Her aunt would lift her T-shirt and they'd both have a laugh.

Mary was mortified. If only she hadn't recorded that last fight, she would still be with her mother. It was okay that her mother killed him, he deserved it. But it wasn't okay for her to wind up with her low-life relatives who despised her and her mother.

And when her uncle came into her room smelling of beer and whisky, she knew what she had to do to protect herself. The knife she kept under her mattress was similar to the one her mother had used.

These brothers had no respect for women.

THE CHILDREN'S EXCHANGE PARK

Augusta and Mary Lee's son, Damon, was a screamer. He didn't just yell or holler when he got upset, he let out a high-pitched scream that lasted longer than a normal child's full breath, and it could continue for excruciating minutes, and that got on his father's nerves. The boy's screams, for reasons obscure to his parents, kept Augusta awake at night and often ruined his mornings when Damon woke up before dawn and screamed to get out of his bed.

Augusta wondered why most other children his son's age seemed less frantic than his son, why they listened to their parents when they ate at restaurants or played at the park. His little boy made too many demands, and he questioned if Perhaps Damon's *enfant terrible* behavior was a result of faulty parenting.

"He doesn't listen," Augusta complained to his wife.

"What child does at his age?" she asked.

"But he does the opposite of what I say. It's like he's testing me."

"He's seeing where his boundaries are."

"Does that include his tantrums?"

"Of course."

"What about the toys he destroys?"

"Kids like to be in control of things."

"The animals he hurts?"

"When has he done that?"

"He hit our neighbor's puppy."

"He was playing with the dog. He was excited."

"What about how he clogs the toilet with toilet paper?"

"He's learning to use the bathroom by himself."

"He bites people."

"Only when he's provoked."

"You've got an answer for all his shitty behavior."

"That's a terrible thing to say. He's a normal four-year-old. You're just a grouchy dad who needs to be in control, and you've met your match."

Perhaps he had, Augusta thought when he took Damon to the playground one afternoon. At the basketball court, there was one basket that was lowered so that smaller children could shoot without getting frustrated. Damon liked to throw his small ball up over his head, most often behind him, and when Augusta tried to show him how to throw the ball in front of him, Damon just walked away. They went to the soccer field, where Damon refused to kick the ball into the net, but instead would pick it up with both hands and throw it behind the net. His father tried to teach him to kick the ball, but Damon would take it and walk away. At the bocce court Damon wouldn't even try to roll his ball but instead wanted to play hide-and-seek. Then he took the sunscreen from the bag in his stroller and squeezed half the tube onto the pavement.

"You're driving me crazy!" Augusta yelled, making Damon cry.

"I want Mommy," he said.

"I want a new kid," Augusta said. He looked around the playground at some of the other kids who were crying or running around unsupervised and had a brainstorm.

What if you could take a break from your kid? What if you could replace your kid with another kid, just for a few days, or a week? That's when he came up with the idea of creating a park for parents like himself, who wondered if the grass was greener on the other side. He appeared before the city's Parks & Recreational Council and convinced the city to provide the land and fund the Tuscaloosa Children's Exchange Park, where parents who were fed up with their child's behavior could make an exchange with other parents fed up with theirs.

It sounded ridiculous, since only parents at their wit's end would want to unload their kid for a while, but it wasn't ridiculous at all. In the first month alone, over a hundred parents had registered their children. Augusta Lee, who was a descendant of General Robert E. Lee, became the focus of a controversial program that riled the media, but had a positive effect on those parents who participated.

The effect on the children, however, remained to be seen. Perhaps in the long run it might prove to be positive, but when these youngsters were put in different homes, they rebelled in any way they could. Damon screamed so loud his new, temporary parents stuck him in front of the television and went into the garage to hit the Dewar's. Other children outdid themselves breaking glass tables, running through screen doors, throwing wooden toys at pets, or going numb. It was obviously traumatic for children under five to be placed in such foster home-like situations, especially when they suspected that their parents were trying to replace them. The end result of these switches was that the majority of participating parents were relieved to get rid of the replacement child and happy to have their own little monster back. Thus, the exchange program was deemed a success because it brought families together. The grass, these parents came to realize, was not greener but disturbingly brown on the outside.

When the children returned home, they showed evidence of insecurities that hadn't been displayed before they were exchanged. They weren't as rebellious or naughty or unnerving as they had been before they left. They had returned to what was familiar, and their separation had shown them to appreciate what they had. How this experiment would change their psyches over the years was yet to be determined, but the program worked as a kind of sedative for a while, and that was a respite for the parents. In twelve months, over six hundred families had participated in the program. The Parks & Recreation committee considered it a qualified success and on the first-year anniversary the members decided a celebration/dedication was in order.

And so, it came to pass that the local media was invited to the renaming ceremony, as Augusta Lee proudly announced that the Tuscaloosa, Alabama, Children's Exchange Park would now be called the Donald J. Trump Children's Exchange Park in honor of the president who understood, better than any president before him, the value of separating children from their parents.

A little separation, Trump had championed, wasn't necessarily harmful, and it might even be beneficial to both the parents and the child. After all, everybody needs a break once in a while.

PHOTO OP

July 3, 2020 President Trump Visits Mt. Rushmore in South Dakota on Indian land to celebrate Independence Day. Fireworks, and 7500 Trumpers without masks or distancing dare the Corona virus to infect them.

"**W**haddya gonna do if this virus doesn't go away by the fall?" Donald Trump's reflection in his bathroom mirror asked as The Donald wiped his face with an alcohol-soaked cotton ball.

"It's going to disappear, and even if it doesn't, I'm making sure the Market's going to go through the roof."

"Not all voters are invested," The Donald's reflection pointed out.

"It's all about the economy. The other shit's not going to matter."

"Where are you planning on planting your name just in case?"

"Yeah, that's been on my mind a lot," The Donald said, picking up his phone and speed dialing Steve Bannon's private line.

"Steve, where you are? I don't care, just get over here, I'm in my bedroom. I want to talk about my immortality."

The Donald pointed a finger at himself in the mirror. "Steve's on his way. I'll show you!" he said.

Before Bannon arrived, The Donald put back on the makeup he had just removed, indicating that this was a meeting he was taking seriously. The polls were showing that he wasn't handling his office as presidentially as he thought he was, and Bannon was just the guy who could help keep him where he belonged, at the top, where no one could touch him.

"Looking good," Steve Bannon said when he walked into the president's bedroom.

"You look like shit," The Donald said. "Why don't you shave? And you could wear a tie once in a while, and maybe real shoes instead of sneakers."

"Don't want to compete with you, sir. When we're photographed together, no one looks at me. I'm not Kanye West."

"He's not a Black Life Matters guy, you think?"

"He's above his color."

"Good man, Kanye. Talks crazy, but he's a supporter."

"Not so sure anymore. He just tweeted that he's running against you this year."

"Yeah, he called me about that. I thought it was a good idea, it will divert 20% of the black vote away from Biden. Not gonna hurt me."

"You never fail to surprise, sir."

"What's with the 'sir'? Since when?"

"Since I left, I noticed you liked to quote others calling you that, so I'm on board with it."

"Look, don't get me off track here, I called you in because it's possible the polls, all the ones I'm suing, might .... well, fuck, what do you think? Am I going to lose this thing?"

"A lot of people are dying, sir. People are wondering why you aren't on the same page as Fauci."

"Fucking guy's not a team player. I'll fire him tomorrow."

"He's still popular, sir. I'd hold off on that for a while."

"Look, Steve, the Wall's not going to be finished by the end of the year. It's not going to look good if it's not completed. I'm going to be remembered for that."

"The Wall is one of your great achievements. I agree, it should get done."

"So, I've been thinking. What if we put a name on the top of the Wall, like every fifty miles? TRUMP, in big letters like the Hollywood sign?"

"Might be a bit much, but not out of the question, sir. Maybe start with your name on plaques drilled into the wall, placed every twenty-five miles. It *is* your wall, deserves your name."

"Yeah, we can start with that. I'll get what's-his-name on it. Mulvaney."

"It's Meadows now."

"Right. Mick Meadows. I'll talk to him about it tomorrow."

"It's Mark," Bannon said. "Mulvaney is Mick."

"How am I expected to remember these guys with the same goddamn initials? The only double M's worth remembering are Marilyn and Mantle. God, The Mick had a sweet swing, didn't he?"

"He sure did, sir."

"You think Netanyahu will pay me back for keeping him in office?"

"What are you thinking?"

"What if TRUMP, in gold, sits atop the Wailing Wall? We'd pay for it, of course."

"That much gold would be pretty expensive," Bannon cautioned.

"I'm not paying," The Donald laughed. "The Treasury will pay for it."

Bannon smiled. "For a moment there I thought you were going to say Mexico."

"Don't laugh, Steve. I don't like to be laughed at."

"I think your name belongs on the Wailing Wall, sir. Fuck, why not? You moved the Embassy to Jerusalem. They've named streets and villages after you. Why not their Wall?"

"So, listen, you know the oil pipeline I got built from Canada. I don't see any credit given. I was thinking about giant steel billboards, maybe every hundred miles."

"With just your name, or should it say something?"

"It's gotta say something; Christ, what's the point of getting credit if you aren't showing what's being credited. Credited or Created? Both, I guess."

"It's a great pipeline."

"Hasn't busted once, has it? Obama was such a pussy. What do you think of these Confederate statues being destroyed? Don't tell me what you think, I'll tell you what I think. It's a fucking shame to destroy them. Here's what might be done; you take the heads off some of these guys, the really bad ones, not the slave owners, they all owned slaves, but the ones who beat the shit out of their slaves, the bad apples, take their heads and replace them."

"With whom did you have in mind to sit on those horses or stand on their pedestals?"

The Donald looked at his former chief advisor and now his unofficial chief advisor and furrowed his brow.

"Ah, yes, why not," Bannon said. "It would save a lot of money and bronze to just put your head on statues that already exist. Good idea, sir. And you're loved in the South, so that might be a no-brainer."

"These things should be done, don't you think? That's why I need to get re-elected, to make sure I get the credit I deserve."

"Even if you don't—get re-elected, I mean—it's not your fault an invisible virus came along and fucked things up around the world. Probably a good thing to get on all these legacy moves now, before the election."

"What about the No Man's Land between North and South Korea? I'm the first president to step foot across it."

"A plaque?"

"A statue. That one deserves a statue."

"Maybe take one of the Confederate ones with your head attached and send it over."

"Not a bad idea. On a horse, you think, or just standing with a sword?"

"Let them choose."

"Yeah, as long as we get the right sculptor for the head. And speaking of heads, you know I'm going to South Dakota for the Fourth of July."

"On the third, yes."

"I was looking at the four heads on Mt. Rushmore. I've asked the White House photographer to make sure he gets shots of me on either side, to the right of Washington and to the left of Lincoln. I think there's room on either side for another president."

"That's a very important monument," Bannon said. "It's kind of the Holy Grail of presidential monuments when you think about it."

"Do you think Mitch McConnell can get a bill through the Senate in time?"

"Worth a try, sir. You certainly belong up there. There's never been a president like you."

"It's got great photo op possibilities. The fake news can't help but run with it. The right picture will plant the seed."

"And if the logistics can't work out there, then maybe you could replace the unfinished monument to Crazy Horse being built into a mountain in South Dakota. It started in 1948 and may never get done. Your supporters could easily raise the money to finish it, if they change it from a crazy Indian to the greatest American president besides Lincoln."

"I wouldn't mind a stand-alone monument, Steve, that's good thinking. But Rushmore's the place. That's the one to go for. And I'm not sure you're right about Lincoln. He made some mistakes, you know."

"You've got a lot left on your plate until the end of the year," Bannon said.

"I'm the president. Somebody's got to take care of this. By the way, how's the TV network shaping up?"

"We've got commitments from Hannity, Ingraham and Tucker already. And O'Reilly wants in as well. *Trump TV* will be the biggest cable startup since CNN."

"That's what we'll do in 2024 then."

"Absolutely. And if it really looks dicey in the fall before the election, we've still got that option for you to drop out, hand it over to Pence for the last few months, and he'll give you that pardon you'll need to start *Trump TV* next year. So, looks like you're in a win-win."

"That's how I see it, too, Steve. Winning is the only way to go."

HELL

Hell was preparing for a celebration.

For over 2,000 years Satan's three mouths sucked on Brutus, Cassius, and Judas Iscariot until, by the mid-21st century, He felt like He had sucked them dry and decided to stick them headfirst in the frozen lake of the Ninth Circle, where they would feel the sensation of drowning without ever losing consciousness. All the denizens of Hell were in a frenzy trying to guess whom Satan would choose to suck on as He sat on his fiery throne in the center of the very bottom of Hell.

"It's got to be Hitler," the Countess Elizabeth Bathory said to King Leopold II.

"You too might be in the running," said the Belgian king, who savagely murdered ten million Congolese. "I may have cut off the hands of those I enslaved, but there are very few among us who bathed in the blood of virgins to maintain their youth."

"I don't have a chance," the Countess replied. "Not with the likes of you, Stalin, Pol Pot, Vlad the Impaler, Ivan the Terrible, and Atilla the Hun. I'd just be an hors d'oeuvre to Satan. A mere canape for his palette."

"My guess is Putin, Kim Jung-il, and Bernie Madoff," chimed in Cincinnati Reds' Pete Rose, who bet on baseball. "All fresh meat for His Eminent Darkness."

"Bernie Madoff, the embezzler, over Talaat Pasha, the leader of the Young Turks and the Armenian Genocide? Or Genghis Khan, who created the Mongol Empire by killing all his enemies?" Brett Kavanaugh cried out, his throat bone dry from all the beer that surrounded him but was inaccessible to him.

"I'll tell you who he'll pick," the rocker Ted Nugent said, "Hillary Clinton, Marie Curie, and that pedophile Jeffrey Epstein."

"I don't even know why Hillary's down here," Clarence Thomas said, exhausted from spitting out pubic hairs that tickled his lips every twenty seconds, which kept him from ever sleeping. "Just because she didn't go to Wisconsin or Michigan, that seems a pretty harsh punishment."

"Pretty petty if you ask me," Heinrich Himmler said. "She belongs with the angels compared to me. I designed Adolph's Final Solution. I should be among the chosen."

"Yeah, maybe," said Donald Trump. "Unless the Holocaust was a hoax. Then you're nothing but background noise. If Satan's choosing among the billions down here, nobody's a better choice than me. I've got the best brain, I know the most words, I've never given anyone credit for anything."

Satan looked among those in the last three rings of Violence, Fraud, and Treachery to see who might replace Judas, Brutus, and Cassius. There were so many prospects, and though some were centuries-old inhabitants, there was something to be said about the new blood that had come down. From just the United States alone there were some of the great sycophants, like Mike Pence, Jim Jordan, Ron

DeSantis, Susan Collins, Lindsay Graham, Rudy Giuliani, Mike Pompeo and Devin Nunes — all Republicans, all despicable, all deserving of their positions in the Underworld. But then there were those guys from Turkey, Syria, China, Israel, Hungary — Erdogan, al-Assad, Xi Jinping, Netanyahu, Ader — all bad, all evil, all worthy of consideration.

Satan enjoyed how all those frying and freezing tried to outguess each other when it came to imagine which three would wind up being devoured and spit up, over and over for thousands of years, before their putrid tastes became bland and He'd have to choose new ones. So many contenders, and yet He knew as soon as they passed the Gate and Dante handed them their tickets to the Ninth Ring of Treachery that it had to be the Trumper Trio — Mitch McConnell, Sean Hannity, and Jared Kushner — who belonged with God's one true nemesis, who sat, licking His three-headed chops, choosing them over that orange-faced, combed-over 45th president whom He relegated to float between the Second Ring of Lust, the Third Ring of Gluttony, and the Fourth of Greed.

This infuriated the man who called himself The Donald, because nothing got him more upset than knowing that any of the men he worked with got more attention than he got. And not being chosen by Satan was thrice as upsetting as anything Nancy Pelosi, Adam Schiff or Chuck Schumer tried to do to undermine him when he was president.

When he tried to set up a meeting with Satan to discuss this slight, he couldn't get past the three-horned goat guards, who continuously poked him with their fire sticks to pay the penance for being such a horny, gluttonous, greedy fellow.

"Do you know who I am?" he would shout each day for the rest of eternity, as he kept trying to get past the guards, making even the dour Hitler and Clarence Thomas chuckle. "This is fucking hell! Why Jared over me? He's a Jew, he couldn't help the things he did. I did shit just for the hell of it. I *belong* with Satan. Nobody didn't care about everything as much as I didn't care. No one else could have single-handedly destroyed democracy, and had You given me a second term, I would have. Who else could have thought of putting such incompetents into place to slow down the post office, to rig the ballot boxes, to bring in armed forces to stir up peaceful protests? Jared fucked up everything I gave him, but it was me who gave all of that to him. Okay, I get why Mitch is there, can't argue with that, but Sean was my puppet; he called me every night and I told him what to say. I gave Rush the Medal of Freedom; how much more did I have to do to earn a place in Satan's mouth?"

Stalin, Pol Pot, and Hitler heard about Trump's whining from their respected places in the Seventh Ring, the ring of Violence, and laughed out loud that such a man who couldn't even make it past the Fourth Ring believed he belonged in the very center of Hell.

"What a stupid, evil man," Pot said to Saddam Hussein, who nodded in agreement, as did Osama bin Laden and Muammar al-Ghaddafi.

"He needs his own separate ring of Ego Maniac," the flesh-eater Jeffrey Dahmer told the clown-faced killer Wayne Gacy. "He never understood himself, so he doesn't appreciate his placement."

"Truly," said the hunchback Richard III, "he never even put a sword through anyone's heart. What'd he do? Put immigrant children in cages? He didn't inject them with the plague, did he?"

"But he did kill hundreds of thousands with his mishandling of the Corona virus pandemic," Typhoid Mary pointed out.

"That's nothing compared to all those I killed," said Genghis Khan, "Eleven percent of the world's population, and I'm stuck in the Seventh Ring."

"As are we," chimed in Stalin, Vlad, Leopold II and Rush Limbaugh.

"An amateur when it comes to pure evil," said Heinrich Himmler. "I was a great architect of evil. Trump was just a pisher."

It was a great celebration in Hell when Satan announced the three who would get as close to Him as any dead or demon could get. They would never be able to bask in their glory because they would have to endure Satan's breath, a breath so foul that all the rotten meat and fish that ever existed, combined over the centuries from the beginning of earthly rot, was like ambrosia compared to what came in and out of Satan's three mouths. But that would never stop Donald J. Trump from wanting to be where few dead ever went. The Donald had convinced himself that he was not just "Among the Chosen," but was "The Chosen" himself. And when he couldn't get past the Fourth Ring, he looked for all the lawyers who had served him, he screamed out for Roy Cohn, and he threatened to sue Satan. But no one listened to him. No one cared what he had to say. Not even when he blasphemed that Hell was a hoax, and that his being bypassed for Mitch, Sean and Jared was rigged.

"Who's Satan, anyway?" he asked every goat demon that poked him. "He may be evil, but I've known a lot of evil people. Bill Barr was evil. Steve Bannon. Ivanka. I know evil. I *fathered* evil. Satan's not that great."

"Maybe, maybe not," shrugged Satan when he heard of The Donald's complaint. "It is what it is."

GRIEVANCES

In the waiting room, Bluto chuckled when he overheard Homer Simpson warning Bart that if he talked about the throat choking, he'd get a doozy when they got home. Popeye seemed curious at what made Bluto chuckle, because he was there to find out why Bluto had no sense of humor. Olive Oyl sat between them because she wanted to delve below her surface to understand why she brought out the beast in Bluto and the fawning in Popeye. Daffy Duck thought the way Popeye and Bluto were both blotto over Olive was hilarious, since it was obvious that she loved neither of them, and Daffy's ridicule pissed off Elmore Fudd, and that's why they were there. Eric Cartman didn't understand why Kyle Broflovski wanted to get to the bottom of the fat ass's anti-Semitism, but if it was a way to get out of school, he was game. Grandma held Tweety's cage in her lap as Sylvester sat next to her, salivating at the yellow morsel that he was never able to swallow. Cinderella was there with her stepmother, Lady Tremaine, hoping to fathom why that cold-hearted woman tore up her ballroom dress and couldn't accept her as a loving daughter. It was a full room, as they all waited for the Roadrunner and Wile E. Coyote to finish their session.

The doctor had a difficult time with those two, as they couldn't sit still for more than twenty seconds. Wile E.

always had the same complaint, that he was sick and tired of falling from great heights or having a boulder smash him flat. The Roadrunner thought nothing of such whining, as Wile E. always managed to survive what should have killed him.

"Hey folks," Bugs Bunny said as he walked into the waiting room looking for an empty chair, "what's up?"

"What's up? You're up!" Yosemite Sam blustered right behind him. "Your time is up, Bugs."

"Yeah, well, Doc, if that's so, why'd you come? We're here as a couple, Doc."

"I'll cap you with a couple of buckshot, you ornery rabbit."

"Don't get your tits all twisted," Bugs said, tweaking Sam's overgrown mustache. "The shrink will shrink you even shorter than you already are."

"Hey Bugs," Daffy said, "I'm here with your shotgun-blasting funny-talking Fudd. Wanna trade nemeses?"

"Okay with me, Daf, but I think Yosemite doesn't have it in for you the way he does for me."

"And I've had enough of you, you scwewy wabbit," Elmer Fudd said, lifting his shotgun.

"Now, now boys," Grandma said. "This is a place to air your grievances safely."

"Aw," said Homer Simpson, "We come for the free donuts."

As Homer began to drool, the Roadrunner emerged from the doctor's office, with Wile E. Coyote behind them. You had to look without blinking, as they disappeared as fast as they appeared, with one chasing the other as usual. The doctor stood by his open door and sighed. They were a very difficult duo to psychoanalyze.

"Who's next?" the doctor asked, assaying the room with the dread of a man who knew that no matter how often he attempted to get into the minds of these characters, they'd never set down their grievances and walk hand-in-hand into the sunset.

"I believe the Jew would like to go next," Cartman said, "so he can suck my balls without being judged by a talking rabbit, a hare-lipped duck, and a tuxedo cat who doesn't know the meaning of *succotash*."

"You can't stop being a dick, can you, Fat Ass?" Kyle said.

"Who's got a harelip, you no-neck balloon face?" Daffy sputtered. "Why, youuuu're deththpicable!"

"Heya-yuck-yuck-yuck-yuck," Popeye chuckled.

"Don't make fun of those little boys," Olive Oyl said.

"Yeah," chimed Bluto. "I'll sock you one."

"Maybe you should put a sock over your mouth instead," Popeye said as an aside.

"Whad'd ya say, ya one-eyed runt?" Bluto demanded, getting up to sock Popeye in his good eye.

"Boys, boys, we're here to get analyzed, not to keep fighting," Olive said.

But boys will be boys and men will be men and rabbits and ducks and cats and birds will be ....

Bam! Wham! Bluto punched Popeye across the room, narrowly missing the doctor, who withdrew behind the door to his office. Grandma dropped her birdcage and Tweety flew out, which sent Sylvester into a frenzy trying to catch him. Bugs moved off to the side to chomp on a carrot and observe the chaos. Daffy grabbed Elmer Fudd's shotgun to use the barrel as a microphone and began announcing the disorder in play-by-play fashion. They had all come to work out their grievances, but it turned into a free-for-all instead.

Popeye popped out the can of spinach he had hidden below his belt and muscled up with two gulps of the leafy green. Their fight was on.

Bluto swung a wild right that Popeye ducked but Elmer Fudd caught. Popeye corkscrewed his football-sized forearm and let loose a blow that sent Bluto crushing into Sylvester, flattening the cat. Lady Tremaine stood up and kicked Grandma, who was trying to shield Cinderella from Olive Oyl's martial arts moves. Yosemite Sam couldn't stand not knowing who to shoot, so he took out his six-guns and sprayed the room with bullets. When the smoke cleared, Sam stood holding his empty pistols with Tweety Bird hiding in his 'stache. The waiting room was crimson with blood. There would be no grievances analyzed this day.

It was a massacre.

DREAMERS

SOY FUTURES

"**W**hat's this?"

Found behind a stack of magazines and worn paperbacks on top of the antique bookcase. A dark suede box three-and-a-half by two-and-a-half inches with a silver push button. The word Widex imprinted between white stitching.

"Oh, that's where I put it. Ha, never would have found that."

"What's in it?"

"Open it."

Two one-inch flesh-colored plastic squiggles on a bed of black velvet.

"What the hell?"

"My mother's hearing aids. She got them a few months before she died. I didn't know what to do with them. Couldn't just toss them; they were expensive."

"They don't look very comfortable."

"They were fitted for her ears. I thought if I ever needed some, they might fit. It *was* my mother's."

"Did you try them?"

"Never did. Never needed to."

"To see if they fit?"

"Not then. Too soon."

"It's been seven years."

"Yeah, now I could. But I hear okay."

"To see if they fit."

"Yeah."

He put one in his ear. It didn't fit at first, until he moved it around.

"Say something."

"What do you want me to say?"

"Doesn't do anything."

"Are there even batteries in them?"

Checking. A tiny flat battery in each. At least seven years old.

"Gotta be dead."

"Ya think?"

"Maybe I'll get some."

"What for? Waste of money."

"See if they work."

Scott Googled the company, saw that there were a few updated versions, but the ones his mother had owned cost $1,400. Got good reviews. Ordered ten packs of HearPro 312 batteries, 1.45 v, six to a pack on Amazon for $21.99. Only wanted two, but seems they only last a week or two, and they weren't sold by individual packs. Thought: probably should have gone to an audiologist to see if Mom's aids were still good. But why wouldn't they be? They were still under warranty when she died. And for what she paid…. Amazon had dozens for under fifty bucks.

Prime brought them the next day.

"Why'd you buy so many?" his wife asked.

"They don't last."

"So what, you don't need them. And no one else will ever use them, that's for damn sure."

"What if they fit you?"

"Your mom and I, we didn't exactly get along."

"Why do you say that?"

"Because we didn't."

"She loved you, in her way."

"She loved you, even if she thought you were a fuck-up. I was in her way."

"Nonsense."

"You always had a blind spot when it came to her."

"We hardly saw her until she got sick."

"And what happened to all her money? We never saw any."

"You know what happened. Her broker said it was tied up in stocks."

"So, what happened to the stocks?"

"She didn't trust her broker. That's why he had to get her certificates, so she always knew what she had."

"So, what … her broker took them?"

"She had them. That's what she told me."

"And …?"

"And they're gone."

"Hell of a system she had."

"She didn't trust people."

"Not even you, apparently."

"Not true."

"Then why didn't she let you know where they were?"

"I don't think she planned on dying."

"She made funeral plans. You'd think she might have left some mention in her will."

"Why rehash this, Janet? What's done is done. We looked for them. We had her safety deposit box opened. We went through her papers. There was nothing. Maybe she gave them away."

"A likely story."

"Could have happened. My grandfather did that when he became senile. Used to take walks and give things away. His watch. His jacket. The money in his wallet. To strangers. It happens."

"So, your mother handed out stock certificates to her helpers? The cleaning lady? The nurses? The plumber?"

"Wouldn't surprise me."

That night, Scott sat alone in the backyard with a glass of bourbon, put the batteries into the Widex hearing aids, and stuck them in his ears. It was a quiet evening, just the steady hum of insects. Hard to tell if such sounds were enhanced. But then, after he had adjusted to the aids, he heard what sounded like a whisper. He could make out the word "Look." It was a woman's voice, faint but distinguishable. His mother's voice. "Look…. under …"

He put his drink down and stared at the pine trees. "Look under." Look under what? He strained to hear more. He shut his eyes tight, creased his face, rocked in his chair.

"Mom? Is that you? Look under what? What are you trying to say?"

He listened harder. He hadn't drunk enough to be hearing things. He felt a chill, even though it was a warm evening. It was definitely her voice. He wasn't hallucinating.

They were her hearing aids. In his ears. It didn't make sense, but there it was. His mother, whispering in his ears. Getting inside his head. "Under what, Mom? Under what?"

"The floorboards. Look ... under ... the floorboards."

"What floorboards? Where? Mom. Ma. Mom."

No answer. No whisper. What she wanted to say she had said. Had she waited seven years to tell him this? Why didn't he try out the aids right away? Why had he waited so long? Why did he keep them? Had to be a reason. He must have known, subconsciously, that they would be a connection to her.

Or .... was he just hearing things? She struggled to get the words out but was very specific. If she was waiting all these years to tell him something, and if this was the some-thing she had waited to tell, then it had to *be* something.

Janet thought she knew.

"That's where she hid the certificates."

"How do you jump so quickly to that conclusion?"

"What else could it be?"

"I shouldn't have told you."

"Why not? We searched her house, couldn't find any-thing. She lived alone. She didn't have dementia. Makes sense to me."

"Someone else lives there."

"Guess we'll need a plan."

In bed, with the lights out, she told him that his mother once said that she didn't want her to marry him. "She didn't think I was good enough for you."

"I don't believe you. If she said that, you would have told me. Or she would have said something to me."

"I'm sure she said something to you."

"She said what she always said about me, what you said she said about me. What else did she say?"

"She offered to pay for an apartment if I left you."

"You're crazy."

"True. I think it was a religious thing. Me not being Catholic. She believed in Christ as her Savior, didn't she?"

"She did."

"And she wasn't pleased that you didn't."

"I didn't before I met you."

"Guess she wanted someone who would convince you otherwise. Bring you back to the fold."

"She was always nice to you."

"She was. I'm just saying this happened before."

"So, now what?"

"I think you put her hearing aids back in your ears tomorrow and see what happens."

He did. His mother's whisper was stronger. "Look under the floorboards." That's all she said. He gave the aids to Janet to listen, but she heard nothing. The message was for him. She believed that. More than he did.

"It's got to be the house," Janet said.

"Probably."

"Let's go, see if that couple still live there."

"Then what?"

"Then we figure out what floorboards."

"Actually, I think I know. The hall closet."

"Why there?"

"I remember that there was a loose board. I used to keep my sneakers there. Never thought of doing anything about it."

"Place to start, then."

"But how to get into the house?"

They drove the ninety miles to where his mother once lived. It was early afternoon and a car was in the driveway. Janet joked that they were on a stakeout.

"Let's just go ring the bell," Scott said.

"Then what? Ask if we can check out their closet, tear up the floor? Let's just sit and wait for them to come out, get in their car, and drive to the market or wherever."

"You want to break into the house when they're gone?"

"If we have to."

"Actually, if they haven't changed the sliding glass door in the back, I used to be able to wiggle it back-and-forth until it unlocked."

"There you go. They leave, we're in and out before they return."

"What if it's not the hall closet?"

"Then we come back with a bigger crowbar."

"Very funny."

No one left the house, so they went to a nearby motel for the night. Up early the next morning to continue their stakeout. Two hours later, the door opened.

"Look, they're coming out," Janet said

The couple got into their car and drove away.

"Showtime!"

Just as he had hoped, the backyard glass door unlocked after a few pulls. They were in. And sure enough, the loose floorboard was as he remembered it. No one had bothered to fix it.

"Use the crowbar," Janet said.

"I'm doing it."

One board lifted, then a second. Beneath the floor, Mom's whispered command proved her son was not going mad. He lifted a metal box from where it was hidden all these years and handed it to Janet. He put the two boards back as best he could.

"Hurry."

"I'm right behind you."

They got to their car, drove to a nearby diner, ordered breakfast. And opened the box.

"There you go," said Janet. "I told you." She shuffled quickly among the stock certificates, hundreds of shares of Microsoft, Amlin, Berkshire Hathaway, Eaton Vance Corporation, and Hasbro, all purchased in the eighties.

"Holy shit! Do you have any idea what these are worth?"

"A hell of a lot more than what she paid for them."

An understatement. The shares had multiplied over and over, as had the prices. What his mother might have paid fifteen or twenty thousand for was easily worth more than a million. And it was theirs, all because Janet had found the hearing aids and Scott had the good sense to buy new batteries.

"Let's bring these to my cousin Maxie. He'll know their value."

"You trust him?"

"He's a broker, so no, not really. But after he takes his pound of flesh, we'll get the bulk."

"Let's not jump the gun," Janet said, carefully placing the certificates back in the box. "Let's just go home and think about this."

That night, Scott sat in his backyard, drink in hand, the small suede Widex box in his lap. "Mom," he said, looking up at the clouds, "you came through. Sorry it took so long for me to hear you."

He opened the box and put the aids in his ears. For a while, he heard nothing more than the crickets chirping. Then, her whisper. "Soy."

"Ma? Say what?"

"Soy … futures."

"Soy futures? What about soy futures?"

"Put all on soy … futures."

"All? What are you saying? We've got enough, Ma. What do I know about soy futures?"

"Listen to me. Do what I say." He heard her very distinctly, even though he could tell that she was struggling to get her words out. Communicating from The Beyond was obviously not easy, and she had waited seven years to deliver these messages, so they were not to be ignored. She had led them to the certificates. She knew what she was doing then. Why challenge her now? If she could see the future, and the future was soy, then soy it would be.

"You sure you heard her correctly?" Janet asked.

"Clear as a whispered bell."

"All of it? On a bean? Sounds like a fairy tale."

"Even so, Jack climbed the beanstalk and returned with the goose, didn't he?"

"So, the stocks aren't enough of a golden egg?"

"What if we could double it? Triple it? Who knows? Maybe make it ten times what we have. Mom's in another place, a different dimension. If an angel whispered in your ear to take what you have and put it somewhere else, would you push her away?"

"Could be the devil, too."

"But it's not; it's my mother."

When they met with Maxie, he did what he could to dissuade them from cashing in the $1.4 million dollars that the stocks were now worth to put it all on a future speculation. And why soy? Where did that come from? He advised them that if they wanted to speculate, they should spread it around. Keep half, play with the other half. The Chicago Board of Trade listed all the possible futures they might consider.

"No, Maxie, not interested in anything else. We want to ride this out."

"Who gave you this tip?"

"Let's not go there, Maxie. Let's just say it's more than a hunch."

"Scott, listen to me. I'm not one to tell you what to do, but it's my fiduciary responsibility to tell you what *not* to do. And you shouldn't do this. No one can predict the market. Not today, not tomorrow, and not six months in the future. Who knows what could happen to soy? Maybe they'll discover that it causes cancer, and no one should ever eat it or dip their sushi in it. Be reasonable. Janet, talk to him."

"Soy futures is our play, Maxie."

"Jesus Christ, you two. Have you lost your minds?"

"You don't want to make the trade, there are plenty of brokers who will," Scott said. "I just thought you'd appreciate the commission."

"I do, of course I do. And I thank you for coming to see me. But … soy futures? You want to cash in Microsoft and Berkshire Hathaway and the others for soy futures? It makes no sense. You'll make more on the dividends than you might with soy."

Maxie did what they asked. Made a nice commission on the sell and buy. Scott and Janet got what they wanted: over a million dollars of soy future contracts due in five months. They felt comfortable with their decision. Mom had guided them to the certificates and sounded even more certain about what they should do with them. They were just being guided from Above. Who could blame them?

So, when the virus hit China and traveled around the world, infecting millions of people, upsetting the market, curtailing the food chain, and farmers had to destroy their soy crops just when their soy futures came due, Scott and Janet fell into deep despair. Cousin Maxie tried to explain to them how the futures market worked. They had bought so many contracts at one price, and now that the price had sunk to almost nothing, they had no choice but to pay the difference, which used up all their money. It didn't make any sense. Why would his mother do this to them? Was she getting revenge for his marrying Janet against her wishes? Was she trying to remind him what a fuck-up he was and always would be?

They were back where they had started before finding the hearing aids, only now they had changed. They couldn't blame each other because they both believed in what they had done.

Scott sat in his backyard every night for a month with his bourbon and his mother's hearing aids, listening for her whisper. He changed batteries twice, hoping the added energy would bring her to him. But her silence was her rebuke. "Why, Ma?" he whispered into the night. "Why'd you lead us to a fortune only to take it from us? Is this what Heaven is like? Or did you go to Hell and thought you'd get a good laugh at our expense? You screwed up our lives, Ma. If that was your intention, well done." He smiled sardonically at the moon and threw the hearing aids into the garbage bin before entering the house.

The actual blame would come a few weeks later, when the sports world focused on one of the few events that took place half-way around the world, at the running of the first King's Cup in Dubai. Horses from eighteen countries competed for this Cup, and the longshot, paying 40-1, made headlines throughout the land. A Kentucky breeder had brought his untested three-year-old thoroughbred to Dubai, and the horse ran away from the field.

His name was Soy Futures.

YOUNG AGAIN

Everyone, at one time or another, has played the genie game. What if you could rub a magic lamp, release a genie, and be granted three wishes? Most everyone would include at least one of the Big Three: Health, Wealth, and Happiness. Health might come as a wish to regain health or never be sick or cure a sick loved one. Wealth could be in the form of winning the lottery and being set for life or being given a stock tip that was about to burst or getting just enough money to live comfortably for the rest of one's life. Happiness has a lot of branches: personal happiness, family happiness, having children when told that was not in the cards, writing a great novel or making a memorable work of art. The next three most likely would include one of these big ones: World Peace, the End of Hunger and Poverty, and Eternal Life.

But when Truman and Joycelyn had their genie moment, they weren't given a choice, but a proposition. On their fiftieth anniversary, they could go back to their wedding day and do it all over again, only the time would not change. They would both be in their early twenties in the year 2021, not in 1971.

They were, naturally, skeptical.

"What you're saying," Joycelyn asked, "is that we basically get to relive our lives from the time we married. Does that mean that our children and grandchildren don't exist?"

The world would be as it is. Only you will change.

"So," Truman said, "would we know what we now know?"

Not fifty years' worth, no, they were told. *You wouldn't be able to predict the stock market, if that's what you're thinking. You'd just be where you are now, only you'd be young again. You wouldn't be 73, you'd be 23. And you'd have at least fifty years ahead of you, and most likely more.*

It was an interesting proposition, though neither of them believed it.

"Can you give us a glimpse of what it would be like?" Joycelyn asked.

This isn't It's A Wonderful Life, *or* A Christmas Carol, they were told. *If you can remember what you were like when you were 23, that's what it would be like.*

"Would I still be a writer?" Truman asked.

"And I a teacher?" asked Joycelyn

You would get to freely choose your paths. If you could figure out a way to earn a living writing and teaching and want to follow that, yes. But as times have changed, so have professions. Many of the outlets you wrote for, Truman, don't exist today. And with the pandemic, teaching isn't done as much in classrooms as online. But the choice is yours.

The genie making them this offer was not a genie at all. It came in the form of a vision, appearing to them after they swallowed a powerful powder sent to them by a Papua New Guinean shaman they had contacted on the recommendation of their albino Native American guru, who had learned of the shaman from a healer from the Cook Islands.

The voice in the vision came to both of them at the same time, which made them think that there was something going on that they didn't understand but that they couldn't dismiss. They were skeptical, naturally. They didn't really believe that by some shamanistic magic they could shed fifty years and start their adult lives anew. Still, it made them wonder: What if? If they suddenly were 23 again, what would happen to their two daughters and their three grandchildren? Would they vanish?

No, came the voice in their heads, *they would be as they are.*

"But that would make their children older than them. How could that be possible?" asked Joycelyn.

Because anything is possible.

"Isn't playing around with Time and Space theoretical and not actual?" Truman speculated.

It's not just theoretical. It's a leap of faith.

"But what if you change your mind after you leap? Can it be reversed?"

This is a choice, a chance to relive or change the arc of your lives. It's not Ping Pong.

"What about memory? Do fifty years of memory get erased? Can we go back to our youth but retain the wisdom of our experiences?" Truman's reporter instincts made it difficult not to ask such questions.

That's something you will find out if you choose to go back.

When the powder wore off and the voice inside their heads went silent, Truman and Joycelyn realized they hadn't asked how it would work. If they said yes, would they suddenly be transformed to a much earlier version of themselves? Or would they have to go through a process? And who would lead them? Would they have to go to New Guinea to find the shaman?

Their guru told them the answers would come once they made their decision. If they decided not to take up the offer to live an extra fifty years, then the path to get there would not need to be explained. If they agreed to this wondrous gift, they'd be ready for the next step. They were given three days to decide.

"This does seem like an offer we can't refuse," Truman said to his wife.

"You really believe it's possible?" Joycelyn questioned. "I mean, really. We were under the influence."

"We both heard the same voice in our heads. This is something more than mumbo-jumbo. Wouldn't you like to go back to when we were starting out?"

"You mean when we traveled all over the world? Can't do that today. When you made a name for yourself as a journalist? Not much chance of that anymore. When I started teaching at Columbia and then UCLA? Campuses are closed now, and who knows when they'll ever return to the way it was when we were young."

"But wouldn't it be something to be younger than our kids? And to grow up with the grandkids? We've got, what? Another ten, maybe twenty years left? Our joints ache, we're taking a dozen medications, our circulation is poor, we stumble over cracks in the sidewalk, our eyesight is going. As I see it—and I can still see it—this is a no-brainer. We'll be playing tennis, basketball, golf; we'll be able to take long hikes again. We won't have to worry about going somewhere away from an ER. Your tits will rise again, my dick will straighten."

"Your eyes will roam again."

"You know I've only had eyes for you."

"What I know is you've slipped up a few times, which I've overlooked," Joycelyn said.

"You going to go there? Now? When we have a chance for a do-over?"

"Why don't you do it. Let me live out my life the way it was meant to be."

"It can't be just me; it has to be both of us," Truman reminded her. "That's the way it is."

"That seems silly, doesn't it? If it's possible at all, what does it matter if it's one or both of us? I think it's a test."

"What kind of test? If we say no, we don't do it. If we say yes, maybe it works, maybe it doesn't."

"And maybe we die and maybe we don't. Maybe we come back grotesque and not as we once were. You don't know."

"You're right, I don't. And maybe I'd like to find out. I can't believe you're not tempted. That you're not curious."

"Oh, I'm curious," Joycelyn said. "And if they can show me something to make me more of a believer, I might be persuaded. But it's just too risky, too insane, to take such a leap. And besides, think about the world we'd be entering. This world. All the unsolved problems, the environmental catastrophes, the polluted air, the dying species, the virus mutations, the political turmoil. The future looks grim to me."

"Maybe we can help change it. Make the world a better place, not just for our grandkids, but for us, too."

They came to no conclusion after a day of such back-and-forth. On the second day, they took what was left of the powder, hoping to bring back the voice and ask for some demonstration that this was for real.

Water to wine? the voice asked. *A dance on water? Magic tricks? You're being offered what no one has ever been offered. You don't have to sell your soul. You only have to be in agreement.*

"Give us something we can agree upon," Truman said. "Blind faith is okay for bungee jumping or walking across hot stones. But erasing fifty years, what will the world look like fifty years from now, when we'd be the age we are today?"

"Will there even be a world fifty years from now?" Joycelyn asked.

Tomorrow is Day Three, the voice said. *Seek clarity.*

When the powder wore off Truman and Joycelyn thought of talking to their children about this.

"Would it matter what they said?" Joycelyn wondered.

"If they were fine with it, it would."

"Why wouldn't they be? First, because they wouldn't believe it possible. And second, if it was, they wouldn't have to worry about caring for us in the years to come. I'm sure it would be a relief."

"So, you're coming around then?" Truman asked.

"I'm thinking about it."

"Don't think too long. We need to make up our minds by tomorrow."

The morning came with news of a dozen new wild-fires in California; with the failure of a Space X rocket that was headed to Mars; with riots breaking out in Chicago,

Portland, and New York over more police shootings of African-American protestors; and the disappointing results of a Covid-20 vaccine.

"Let's get young again," Truman said. "We can weather this storm."

"Do you really think so?" Joycelyn asked. "Seriously, Tru, do you?"

"I think we should give it a shot."

"And I think it's the last thing I'd want to do. Fifty more years? Of this? Shoot me, instead."

They had until the end of the third day to decide. Fifteen more hours. Truman pulled out the If-You-Love-Me card. Joycelyn countered with More-Than-You-Know.

As the clock wound down.

DOPE

On the 226th day since the Covid-19 virus was declared a pandemic, the day of the last presidential debate between Donald Trump and Joe Biden, Brad Wolendorf ran out of dope. "Dope run," he told his wife Clara. "Want anything?"

"You're the dope," she said. "You're not going anywhere."

"I have to. President Asswipe is going to interrupt his opponent, mock him for wearing a mask, attack his son Hunter, and spew his vile, poisonous, separatist, divisionary words to try and unite his base and create as much chaos as he can. No way I want to miss this, and no way can I watch it without a substantial buzz."

"Now you're going to bring back the virus and blame Trump when you do," Clara said.

"I'll be careful. I'll order curbside. Never leave the car. Wear a mask."

"They don't take credit cards."

"Wrong, they do now."

"Then you gonna sanitize the card after?"

"I could. Or I'll hand over cash, forget any change, and be back before the show begins."

"Why can't you just watch TV like a normal person?"

"When Trump comes on, you leave the room," Brad said. "Is that normal?"

"Of course, it is. What's abnormal is you wanting to listen to what he says."

"That's because he doesn't ever make any sense. He's a master of the theater of the absurd. Just listen to how he mispronounces Ulysses, Minneapolis, and Yosemite. Why else would I watch?"

"You get off on him too much," Clara said. "He's a dangerous, mentally deranged man. He's not funny."

"He's also probably a drug addicted pill popper. But we may be rid of him in three months, so I don't want to miss this last hurrah. He said he might leave the country if he loses. Imagine that! Who would take him? Putin? The Saudis?"

"You shouldn't make fun of the mentally ill."

"You're repeating yourself," Brad said. "Look, I wanted him to run in 2016 because I never thought he'd get the nomination, but I knew he'd spice up the debates, which he did. But then, he fucking became president against all the polls. So, yes, it was no longer a joke and it was a mistake to want him around for my amusement, I admit it. But you've got to at least admit that you never expected to see the Republican Party turn away from whatever principles they once had to blindly follow this Mob Boss Pied Piper. Don't you ever wonder what he holds over them? He's like J. Edgar Hoover with his dossier of shit about everyone in office, only Trump's more criminal than any of them. That's what's so puzzling. He came up with this tweet shit and it became a weapon. He tweets and those who oppose him fall. It's nuts. But it's happening. It's taken an invisible virus to finally expose that he wears no clothes. But there's gotta be some good that's come out of this."

"Good? Trump? Good for nothing, that's what he's good for."

"What about publishing? He's certainly been good for publishers. There are hundreds of books about him and hundreds more coming. Publishers are surviving because of him."

"Who wants to read about such an asshole?"

"Apparently quite a lot of people," Brad said. "And what about the Wall builders? He's good for those workers."

"They could be building housing for the needy instead," Clara said.

"Ratings. He's good for Fox and his base. He's good for MSNBC and CNN for his haters. With higher ratings, they charge more for ads, so his polarizing personality actually boosts the economy. Not to say what it must have done for Sean Hannity's salary. Do you think there'd be a place for a Laura Ingraham or a Jeanine Pirro if it wasn't for Fake News?"

"I can't believe you're trying to find something positive about the biggest criminal that's ever made it to the White House. Nixon was a marshmallow compared to this guy."

"Just because all his best men are now felons doesn't mean he doesn't know the best people."

"Right," Clara said, "he had the best campaign manager, the best national security advisor, the best foreign policy advisor, the best personal lawyer. Where are they now? And all those generals that he claims to know more than, the fucking draft dodger. His own son was going to be disowned if he enlisted. That's your commander in chief."

"Gotta admit, makes for some great comedy," Brad said.

"224,000 dead and counting from a virus that could have been contained with the proper leadership; Russians paying the Taliban to kill our soldiers in Afghanistan; China making inroads with Iran; taking us out of the climate agreement; dropping the World Health Organization during a pandemic; defending white nationalists as very good people; teargassing protestors; separating children from their parents …..he's a riot. But excuse me for the vomit in my mouth that keeps me from laughing."

"See, you leave the room when he comes on, yet he hasn't left you. Maybe that's why he recovered so quickly from the virus—he didn't need protection because maybe he *is* the virus!"

"Enough with Trump already," Clara said, exasperated. "I don't like hearing about him, I don't like seeing him, he turns my stomach. I hate him. I hate him. I *hate* him!"

"That's why you should smoke."

"Bad for your lungs, this virus is a respiratory thing."

"OK, gummies then. Mints. Cookies. I'll get you some."

"I don't need to get stoned to stay mad."

"No, you need it to relax and forget," Brad said. "To laugh again."

"Makes me sleepy. And I can't forget what's happening; if I got stoned, it would only heighten my paranoia. Want me to jump out a window?"

"Hey, I'm not forcing you, just suggesting. You do what you want, but what I want is to stay high, and I can't if I'm out of dope."

"I married a dope."

"Yes, you did. At least, a doper. And thank God for it. You're just lucky I'm not a MAGA."

"If you were, we wouldn't be together."

"People stay together even if they're from different parties."

"Not this people," Clara said. "I'd leave you in a second."

"And where would you go with this pandemic?"

"You're right. I'd kick *you* out."

"Where would I go?"

"To Hell, with the rest of them. Sheep to the slaughter."

"Maybe this never happened," Brad said. "Maybe Hillary won, and we've dreamed this."

"I wish."

"If I were a genie and granted you a wish, would that be it?"

"Knowing what we know now, probably."

"Or .... what?" Brad asked.

"One wish? I thought genies gave three."

"This one gives one."

"I'd have to think about it."

"Do that, while I go to the dope store."

"I wish you wouldn't," Clara said.

HOOKED

Jimmy didn't remember how he got to the screening room, and he didn't know who the people were who were there. He definitely didn't know the young, friendly redhead who sat down next to him after asking if the seat was free. She was all smiles and full of chatter. But Jimmy seemed as if he had lost consciousness for a time and came to in this room. He didn't know if there was going to be a screening, and if there was, what the movie might be. All he knew was that he had a sharp pain at the base of his left thumb. When he looked at his hand, he saw that it was pulsing where the pain was. He stared at his palm, wondering what was going on. The pulsing pushed up the pad of his skin and he knew something was wrong. This wasn't a throbbing nerve; this was something inside his hand trying to get out. He stared, first in curiosity, then in fascination. The young woman next to him was chattering away as if they were old friends, but all Jimmy could do was hold his hand closer to his face until the worm broke the skin, poking its head out, the way the creature in *Alien* came out of John Hurt's chest. It had small antennae and a distinctive little worm face, and when Jimmy looked at his forearm, he could see the worm's body slowly moving below.

He didn't make a scene. He just stood up as the redhead kept talking, his hand held above his bent elbow, and left the darkened room. His initial instinct was to grab the worm's head between the fingers of his right hand and pull, but he suspected that he might tear its head off, leaving its body inside him. He didn't know much about worms, but he knew there were a number of them that could live inside a human body. The tapeworm was probably the most common, and he once read that they could grow up to eighty feet and survive for thirty years in an intestine. There were also thread or pin-worms, roundworms, hookworms and guinea worms, and any one of them might be living inside him at the moment.

He thought that he should get a tweezers and try to pull it out gently. But would it be such a good idea to do it by him-self? Probably should go to an ER. He left the building and looked for a taxi. The worm had retreated, leaving the hole in his palm, and causing Jimmy to wonder how long this worm had been feeding inside him, how he had gotten it, and how much damage it was doing to his body.

He couldn't find a taxi in the rain, so he began to walk, not knowing where the nearest hospital was. When he saw a 24 hour pharmacy, he walked in to see what the pharma-cist had to say.

"Have you been to West Africa lately?" the pharmacist asked him.

"Ten years ago," Jimmy said.

"Well, the guinea worm is the one that breaks through the skin, so that's probably the one you've been hosting."

"I thought that was eradicated."

"Not ten years ago. There are still some cases, but it's much more under control than it was when you were there."

"So, this thing could be ten years inside me?"

"If that's what it is. Some worms are harmless, some cause your ass to itch, and some can chew up your liver or make you blind. Whatever it is, best to get rid of it."

"Any suggestions?"

The pharmacist told him to take a seat and wait to see if the worm reappeared. Once it did, he said, he'd show him how to get it out.

"It's a slow process," he warned. "May take weeks, depending on how long it is. But once you get it started, you'll manage. Pretty painful, though."

Jimmy looked at his hand and wondered how painful it would be. But that didn't matter as much as getting it out did.

He waited nearly an hour, and then the worm stuck its head through the hole in the soft padding of his palm. The pharmacist unwrapped a tampon, pulled the rolled cotton from the plastic applicator, and carefully placed it in Jimmy's palm, close to the worm. "Be still," he said. "Let the little fucker get on the cotton. Once it does, we're going to roll it very gently until we turn him."

"Then what?"

"Then you're going to keep turning, slowly, until it's out."

Jimmy sat down again and waited for the worm to explore the tampon. If he got it when he was in Sierra Leone, it must have been when he crossed a creek wearing an open sandal. Stupid to have done that, he thought. "Hey," he said, "it's on the cotton."

The pharmacist came over and lifted the tampon slightly, turning it like he was winding a watch. The worm stretched as it folded under the rolled cotton.

"Damn!" Jimmy exclaimed. "That fucking hurts!"

"Yeah, I told you it would. But see, it hasn't snapped. It will stretch, and you have to keep turning, very slowly, maybe a half turn every five or ten minutes. It's like catching a big fish, you know? Like a marlin. Only instead of giving it line to run, you have to get it so it can't unroll. Once you've turned it a few times, it will be hooked and eventually come out. You just have to be patient. If you try to pull it too quickly, it will resist and may snap. Then you've got the head but not the body. When you stop turning, it will relax a bit, and that's when you turn a little more."

"How am I going to do this overnight? For weeks?"

"Once you've got a few inches out, he can't go back. So, you can sleep and start rolling again when you wake up. Should get maybe an inch or two then before it starts to resist."

"You sure this is the only way?" Jimmy asked.

"Not the only, but the least damaging. You could always cut into your arm and see if it can be pulled out, but I wouldn't advise it. Go home and Google it. Plenty of pictures to see. Mostly of children crying as it's slowly wound around a stick or a pencil."

Jimmy thanked the pharmacist, cupped his fingers around the tampon, and walked out into the rain. He didn't have an umbrella and kept his left hand in his jacket pocket, stopping at a 7-11 for coffee before continuing on for whatever time it took to make it the two miles to his apartment.

When he got inside, he looked at his palm and turned the cotton a full rotation before the worm resisted.

"Well Bo," he said, "this is going to be fun." He named the worm after the city in Sierra Leone where he thought he picked it up. It was anything but fun, with each turn of the tampon causing excruciating pain. He took three Advils and a hit of sativa oil from his vape pen, wrapped a handkerchief around his hand and went to bed.

In the morning, Bo didn't resist the twisting until an inch and a half came out of Jimmy's palm. When Bo tightened, Jimmy wrapped the handkerchief around his hand again and made himself coffee and cereal for breakfast. Until the worm was out of him, his activities would have to be limited to what he could do with his right hand.

In the evening, he went to a nearby jazz club where he saw the chatty redhead who was at the screening the night before. She recognized him and sat down at his table. "That thing still in your hand?" she asked.

"It is," Jimmy said. "Didn't know you noticed."

"Creepy," she said. "I'm Suzzee"

"One Z or two?"

"Two."

"Y or IE?"

"Double E. Sometimes Y. Depends how I feel."

"With two Z's, you must feel powerful."

"Oh, so you know the power of the Z," Suzzee said.

"Not really, I was joking."

"It's not a joke. Z is the coolest letter in the alphabet."

"And that's because …?"

"It's aggressive, funny, exciting, sharp, incisive. It's awesome."

"What about X?"

"A Z wannabe."

"So, what's the least cool letter?" Jimmy asked.

"H. Nobody really likes H."

"Still, it's a bridge between two lonely I's."

"Could say that. What's the ugliest letter?"

"Have no idea?"

"V."

"You're pretty up on your letters, aren't you?"

"What two letters are the most listened to?"

"Give me five and I'll tell you," Jimmy said.

"CD," Suzzee said and laughed. "Got you."

"Three less than the M, U, S, I, C I was going to say."

"Can I see it?"

"What?"

"The worm. Can I see it?"

"Not much to see," Jimmy said, removing the handkerchief from his hand. "It's rolled up on this."

"Is that a tampon?"

"It is."

"Very clever. Your girlfriend's?"

"No, the pharmacist gave it to me. I just have to keep winding it when it least resists."

"Does it hurt?"

"Only when I turn it."

"Can I try?"

"Seriously?"

"Something new. It's always good to try something new. It's like eating something new. The Japanese say you live longer whenever you eat something you've never eaten before."

"You're full of arcane knowledge, aren't you?"

"Here's one I bet you don't know. What letter followed Z into the 19th century?"

"A?"

"If A is for ampersand, then yes."

"Didn't know that was ever a letter."

"Told you, you wouldn't. Not many people know that."

Jimmy held out his hand and let Suzzee wind the tampon a half turn. "Christ!" he winced. "Fucking thing's like a fire stick."

"How long do you think it is?" Suzzee asked.

"Too long," Jimmy answered.

They looked at each other and, as the jazz trio played "Take the A Train," they bonded. Over a guinea worm.

What she liked about him was how calm he was with the worm inside him; she knew if it were her, she'd be so freaked out she'd need hospitalization and a morphine drip. What he liked about her was that she wasn't at all freaked out by his situation, that she even found it fascinating, making him attractive, even if he never felt that way about himself.

"What was the movie about?" he asked when the music stopped.

"What movie?"

"Last night, the screening room."

"Oh. Some science fiction bullshit, zombies, aliens, I don't know, I didn't pay attention."

"Did you see the whole thing?"

"No, I left when the killing started. It was stupid. Who invited you?"

"I don't know," Jimmy said. "I don't remember going there or what I was doing once I was there. Then this thing punctured my skin and …"

"Yeah, you got up right quickly. I thought you were pretty cool about it. If it were me, I'd have screamed, maybe fainted."

"You don't look like the fainting type."

"I'm not. But then, I never had what you have living inside me. What if it has a brother that comes out your pee hole? Bet you wouldn't be so cool then."

"My pee hole? Now that's a rare use for dick."

"Can you imagine?"

"Now that you've planted that for me, yes, I can. And no, I can't. I mean, that would be too much. But thank you for giving me something to fall asleep to."

"How would you pee if it were coming out of there?"

"Changing the subject, what are you doing here?"

"I know the horn player. Just a friend. You?"

"Just needed to get out of my apartment, take my mind off my little friend."

"Think it's kismet?" Suzzee asked.

"What?"

"Us meeting like this. Last night. Then tonight. I think it is."

"Do you believe in fate?"

"Only if it's positive. I like you, even if you do have worms."

"Worm."

"Well, you don't know, really. Your insides might be crawling with life."

"You can be very cheery, can't you?" Jimmy said.

"Let's go back to your place when the next set is over. We can be cheery together," Suzzee said. Jimmy thought all she needed was a jeweled tooth to make her smile sparkle.

On the walk to his apartment Suzzee asked where Jimmy might have picked up the worm and he told her about a college roommate he once had who was from Sierra Leone. "He invited me to see his country, so I went. And came back with this unexpected souvenir."

"I never wanted to go to Africa. Is that strange?" Suzzee wondered.

"Not that many people have gone. In fact, I read that less than half of all Americans have a passport. I find *that* strange."

"Not if the other half are babies and teenagers."

"They still need one if they're traveling with their parents."

"Traveling's not that safe anymore."

"You should still have a passport. Just in case."

"In case what? Alien invasion?"

"In case you get married in the spur of the moment and want to honeymoon in Paris."

"Now aren't you the romantic. Is that a proposal?"

"Do you have a passport?"

They laughed. Both seemed fine with small talk and silly banter. And even though Jimmy's apartment was less than impressive, and his left hand was useless, they managed to forget all about Bo the worm, alien invasions, and being trapped in America when their lips met, and their bodies joined.

***

Perhaps it was kismet, Jimmy thought after their second week together, when Suzzee invited herself to move in after Bo moved out. Her body felt much better when he was able to feel her with both hands. It didn't surprise her that he knew how to cook because, she told him, he looked the type.

"What type is that?" he wondered.

"The type who knows the difference between linguini and cannelloni."

"Funny, but you don't look like you'd know how to spell either."

"Fuck you, man, I always aced the spelling tests. Just never bothered to learn how to make anything."

"Why we get along so well. I cook, you eat."

"And we both do the dishes."

It had been years since Jimmy had a girlfriend. Had he not stumbled into that screening room—kismet again? —he might never had hooked up with this capricious Suzzee with the fire red hair. Was it a match made to last, or was this just one of her flings? Did she have flings?

She was definitely kinky. When she sucked his cock, she liked to stick a finger up his ass. The first time she did it, Jimmy tightened his sphincter muscle.

"Nobody ever did that to you?" she laughed.

"Guess there's a first time for everything," he said.

The fourth time she did it, she felt something slimy and stopped her sucking just as Jimmy was about to come. "Don't stop," he said.

"Guess what?" she said.

"Not now."

"You've got another one."

"One what?"

"Bo's brother. Or sister. Or twin. I think I can get it. Hold tight."

"You're shitting me, right?"

Suzzee grabbed the slippery fucker between her fingers as Jimmy grimaced, more in disgust than pain.

"Relax," she said as she pulled. "I've got this."

FREEFALLING

Stowaway's Body Lands in London Garden.
Police said the individual fell from a Kenya Airways flight from Nairobi when the landing gear came down. His body was intact because it was an ice block. "This happens once every five years," said a Heathrow official. – BBC, July 2, 2019

When the landing gear began to come down, as the plane slowed to 150 mph and the altitude was at 2,000 feet, Moses Ansah Mwangi started to come to. His body had been curled around the rear wheel in the well. His blood oxygen level was well below normal; his lungs felt like they were collapsing; he was lightheaded, weak, his arms and legs had severe tremors; and he could barely see. The next few minutes would determine whether he might live or die, but only if he managed to stay in the well until the plane landed. If he fell out of the well after the compartment doors re-opened, all his planning, all his hopes and dreams, would almost surely come to an end. A crushingly bad end.

He shook his head to loosen the cobwebs, the acidosis, the hypothermia he had experienced stowed away on this flight from Kenya to the U.K. The wind blew through the compartment with hurricane-like force, pinning his weakened near-frozen body to the wheel well wall. But the descent wasn't smooth; there was turbulence as the plane dived below a thousand feet, tilting the fuselage from left to right.

Moses felt the rush of air accelerating around him as he fell out of the well.

How desperate had Moses' life been, to bring him to risk it in this way? Surely, there must have been some other way to change his life. A move to a different city. A job in a neighboring country. A caravan across the Sahara. All difficult moves, but none as daring, or as dangerous, as stowing away in a wheel well of a jumbo jetliner.

He suffered from anemia and piles. He had dropped out of middle school to help provide for his family. But after he lost his second job in three weeks and his family called him six different names that all pertained to failure, he wasn't exactly feeling on top of the world. But he was nothing if not resilient, and Moses had a plan. He would leave his country and travel to England, where his best friend Samuel was going to school on a scholarship. Once settled in, he would work hard, doing chores the English shunned, and make enough money to return to his family, if not a hero, then at least no longer a failure in their eyes.

Like so many Africans, family was important to him. He knew that people from other continents valued their independence more than their familial ties, but that wasn't so for him. He respected his father and mother, his aunts and uncles, the elders in his village, his older siblings, including his big brother Kwezi, who had taken from him what mattered most. He knew that, had he stayed in his village, he would never amount to much, because his family had shown their disappointment with him, and had already given him nicknames, ones that usually lasted a lifetime. He couldn't bear being called Lunkhead or Squatter Boy or "*Utajua Hujui*," which meant "You'll Know You're Not Smart." But he knew his brain was good and that given the right opportunities, he could put it to use. Going abroad and returning with earned money in his pocket would change the shame he felt being ridiculed by his family. But getting a passport, then a visa, and buying a plane ticket— all of that was out of his reach. No one would sponsor him. And no embassy would grant him a visa unless he was accepted by a school, and he didn't have enough education to advance in that way. Besides, all the money he had saved wasn't even enough to bribe a guard at the airport to let him through the international gates.

He had heard about stowaways who had survived and about some who had not. His friend Sam had written to describe the wonders of London and offered to share his room if he came. So, Moses began to dream, and to go to the airport to assess how he might sneak his way onto the right plane. Twice a week he would stand outside the fence watching how luggage was stored on these jumbo jets. He wondered if he could fit into a steamer trunk and send himself to England, but he realized that luggage had to be checked in by the traveler, so that wouldn't work. He saw how large the landing wheels on these planes were and figured there had to be room for a skinny guy like him. He knew if he could figure out a way to get into the wheel well, he might have a

50-50 chance to make it to London and, the way he thought about his life, that seemed like decent odds.

It took him weeks of observing how the planes were loaded once they rolled into a gate. He would have preferred to sneak onto the tarmac at night, but the nonstop flight to London took off in the morning, so he had to find a way to cut through the fence, wearing a jumpsuit similar to the ones the workers wore, and casually approach the plane, as if he knew what he was doing. His brain was working well, he felt, as he had hatched his plan and carried it out without a hitch.

It took all his strength to shimmy up the landing gear, and there were a few acrobatic moves he had to make. But determination can do wonders and he moved surprisingly well without hurting himself as he climbed over the wheels and into the well. Once there, he tried to figure out where it would be best to stand when the wheels retracted. If he got it wrong, it would all end before the plane left the air-port. But he got it right and, though it was cramped, he had enough room to wiggle his toes and fingers, and even stretch his neck.

The adrenaline rush he felt when the plane took off was unlike anything he had ever experienced, as was the cold that set in as the plane climbed in altitude. To keep his spirits up, he thought about the family he was leaving, and the city to which he was heading. His mother had given birth seven times and had had a very hard life. She loved all her children, he was sure, but she had no time to play with them as they grew up and, being illiterate herself, she couldn't read to them or stress the importance of education. His father worked for an oil company a few hundred miles away from their village, returning twice a year to be with them. He walked with a limp after a rigging had fallen on his leg and they were all grateful that he had escaped certain death if it had fallen on his head or body. His brother Kwezi was the hope of the family, the first to attend secondary school, and a natural charmer who joined a ghetto hip hop band as a singer. Moses always looked up to his brother, styling himself with Kwezi's hand-me-down American jeans, Kangol cap, and Nike sneakers. But when Kwezi took a liking to his girlfriend Zawadi, Moses knew he must do something big to win her back. Zawadi was the daughter of a local commissioner. She and Moses had grown up together, and Moses assumed they would marry when he could afford it, but he knew he couldn't compete with his older, hipper brother, even though he was sure Kwezi was not serious about her.

With his hands and feet numb by the cold, and his body wrapped around a giant rubber wheel, Moses replayed the conversation he had with Zawadi to keep him from passing out. Anger was a strong motivation for heartbreak. And though he didn't show his ire when she told him that she was hooking up with Kwezi, he had felt incredible turmoil boiling inside him. If he could keep that turmoil boiling, he might just make it the eight hours to London. But as the temperature decreased to well below zero, he had a hard time staying angry.

He had so much to prove, so much …. Over and over, he lived through his life as a boy, as a teen, as a young man. He relived the jobs he had failed at. He remembered his mother's cooking. He thought of how he and his best friend Sam hunted for bush rats and small deer. He puckered his lips, imagining he was kissing Zawadi. He heard Kwezi singing and laughing; he saw him looking at Zawadi. He ran these images again and again as his mind distanced itself from his nearly numb body. And when he heard the cranking sound of the landing gear compartment doors opening, he knew it would soon be over, this terribly uncomfortable, disfiguring flight to a better future.

As the landing wheels began to straighten from the cocoon of the compartment and the wind pinned him to the well wall, his body numb, his eyes unable to blink, his thoughts turned towards forgiveness. He forgave his mother for not being as loving as he had wished. He forgave his father for never being there when he needed him. He forgave Kwezi for stealing his girl. And he forgave Zawadi, because he knew that when he returned, she would see him differently and they would have a happy ending. That is what he thought about when the turbulence turned the plane from side to side and up and down, throwing him into the atmosphere above London.

And he flew, like a rocket, to his destination.

SECOND CHANCES

"What are you thinking?"

"About my mother."

"What about her?"

"How she died."

"She didn't suffer long."

"Long enough. It started when she fell, before the cancer. What I was thinking about was the night she died. I should have gotten in bed with her, held her. She was so fragile."

"Maybe she wouldn't have wanted that. She was in pain."

"The morphine helped her pain. And who doesn't want to be held when they're dying? We knew she wouldn't make it through the night."

"Are you feeling guilty about it?"

"Sort of. It's been a while, I know. Why didn't I do that? I remember we were all tired, taking turns sitting up with her, but when it was my turn, I held her hand, but I don't remember hugging her."

"Maybe you did. You probably did."

"Just wish I had a do over on that one. So many things we can do again, make amends, but not with death. You've got one chance, and then you just have to live with it."

"I wish I had done things differently when my mother died. I remember that she kept pointing to something in the kitchen, she wanted something, but I didn't know what. I should have tried harder to understand. I felt so helpless."

"Maybe she wanted ice cream."

"Hah."

Second chances. Would that be a genie wish? To go back in time and do something differently? Or would that be a wasted wish? If you only had one, would it be to hug your mother on her deathbed or get a hundred million dollars tax free? Prevent your father's second stroke or have good health until your death at 110?

Silly questions. You can't go back; you shouldn't look back. Life is life, it's that simple. You make mistakes, you surprise yourself, you laugh, you cry, and then you die. That's what Gabriel thought after thinking about his mother. He also thought about all the stories that took characters back in time or ahead into the future. Where did writers come up with these stories? Were they all tapping into their imaginations? Or could even just one of them have had a true visitation? Not by a Time machine or a magic carpet or with superhuman powers that could reverse time, but by something more profound, something spiritual, or maybe even alien.

On the day Gabriel felt remorse about his mother's death, the earth slipped between the sun and the moon. It may have affected his sleep that night because he had a series of unusual dreams. Each dream brought him back to significant moments of his life, but the outcome of these moments was slightly askew from how they had happened. The first, not surprisingly, was with his mother the night she passed. When he asked her if she would like him to lay down with her, she waved him off. "Mom, let me hold you." She couldn't talk, but she could shake her head. She shook her head. "Mom, I'd give up a hundred million dollars just to hold you for five minutes." She opened her eyes and gave him a puzzled look. When he saw her mouth moving, he put his ear to her lips. "Are you stupid?" she whispered. "No, Ma, you're worth more than that. You're worth all the money in the world." "Shush," she said. "Let me die in peace, and not thinking that I raised a stupid son."

The dream that followed this was about the only time Gabriel had physically punished his twelve-year-old son. The boy had been caught stealing a baseball glove and Gabriel felt he had to leave an impression on his body that he wouldn't forget. He found a tree branch and whipped it twice across the boy's bottom. It hurt Gabriel's psyche more than it did his son's behind, and he could never forgive himself for such abuse. In his dream, it was his son who picked up the switch and whipped Gabriel across his chest, his arms, and his face. When Gabriel sank to his knees, his son kicked him in his head and ran away.

His third dream took place at Yankee Stadium, when Gabriel grabbed a foul ball off the bat of Derek Jeter. A young boy had dropped it from his glove and in the scramble to retrieve it, Gabriel managed to pick it up. The boy looked up, hoping Gabriel would give it to him, but Gabriel said, "I have a kid at home who will want this." In his dream, Gabriel gives the ball to the boy, but then the boy's father punches him for going after the ball in the first place.

When Gabriel awoke the next morning, he felt as though a weight had lifted from his body. When his wife said, at breakfast, that she had been thinking about what they were talking about the day before, Gabriel just smiled. "You mean, second chances? Forget about it. Second chances aren't any better than what you did the first time around. Could even be worse."

His wife couldn't help wondering how he came to this conclusion. "What about that genie wish?" she asked.

"You mean the money or the hug? Take the money," Gabriel said. "Why be stupid about it?"

KILLER DREAMS

T wo old friends were talking about their dreams.

"It's the strangest thing," Simon said, "but I've had this recurring dream where I killed someone when I was a kid and buried his body in a garbage dump."

"How old were you?" Lev asked.

"I don't know. How old were those kids in *Stand by Me*? Like that age."

"It's a movie dream," Lev said. "I've had something like that, too."

"Who'd you kill?"

"I was about eleven. The kid was the same age, I think. Maybe younger. I buried him in the far corner of a park on Ditmas Avenue, near where we used to live. I wonder if that park is still there. It's been sixty years."

"Do you think it's a common dream? Having killed someone?" Simon asked.

"I never thought about it. Sometimes when I dream it, I wake up in a sweat," Lev said.

"Me too. It seems so real. Like I've actually killed someone."

Simon was a rabbi of an orthodox congregation. Lev was a graphic designer. They had known each other since elementary school and remained friends, even though Simon was religious and Lev an atheist. They just didn't let God stand in their way.

"I'm going to put out an email to some of our friends, see if any of them have had a killing dream," Lev said.

"I bet a lot of them have," Simon said, "though they may not admit it."

"Maybe it's one of the iconic dreams, like falling, flying, or drowning."

"Or being chased. Or losing teeth. I've read about those. You think animals have such dreams?" Simon wondered.

"Biting ones, probably. Murder is pretty much a human thing."

"If I'm not mistaken, most people in our dreams are really subconscious versions of ourselves. So, killing someone is really tackling a part of ourselves we don't like."

"Sounds like psychobabble to me," Lev said.

"But since we haven't killed anyone, then maybe it's just our subconscious letting us know that it's okay to have both negative and positive feelings about ourselves. That the two make up the whole. We are who we are, warts and all."

"You got your rabbi shtreimel on?" Lev joked. "You're trying to make sense of something that doesn't make sense."

"Unless you really killed someone, and you can't suppress it from your sleeping mind," Simon said.

"I killed a bird once with a BB gun when I was ten or eleven. I felt awful for days. You ever kill anything?"

"No. But I did flush a goldfish down the toilet. And I once had a guinea pig that died. Buried it in our backyard."

"And then you became a rabbi," Lev said.

"God called."

"And what did He say?"

"'Enough with the flushing and burying. Follow me.'"

The old friends enjoyed each other's company. They could let down the facades life taught them to construct and just be themselves. Simon was the first to get married and have children. When Lev found the right woman, Simon performed the ceremony. Both men made decent livings. When the synagogue needed artwork, Simon made sure Lev got the job. When Simon gave his Friday night sermons, Lev sat in the back and listened, even though he didn't bother to pray. Sometimes Lev took issue with his friend's morality; and sometimes Simon questioned Lev's lack of faith. But nothing either of them did ever altered how they felt about each other. They were like brothers.

Each was convinced that if one needed a favor, the other would comply.

And then, bones were discovered.

It was Simon who found out about them. He happened to be driving past a construction site on Ditmas Avenue, where the park used to be. He remembered Lev saying, in his dream, he had buried the child he killed in the corner of the park. Out of curiosity, Simon parked his car and walked to where a group of workers were huddled in the far corner. They were all looking at something they had uncovered. Bones. The skull and skeleton of a child.

Simon asked one of the workers about the discovery. Nothing was known, other than someone had buried this child, and because the remains were just bones, it must have been a while ago. At least forty or fifty years. Maybe much longer.

"So, what do you do with it?" Simon asked.

The police were on their way, he was told. What they would do, who knew?

When Simon got back to his car, he felt ill. This couldn't be a coincidence, he thought. Lev had just told him about his dream, and now it seemed that it might not have been a dream at all. Could it be possible? Could Lev have done such a thing and suppressed it all these years? Was it something that had been haunting his spirit?

Simon said a prayer. He didn't drive home, but instead drove to Lev's house. This was not something he could keep to himself.

"What are you telling me?" Lev asked when Simon told him.

"Just what I said," Simon repeated. "They found a child's body in the corner of the park where you dreamed you buried it."

"They found a body?"

"They found bones. A skull. The body was picked clean by the insects."

"How do you know it was insects?" Lev asked. "Are you now an authority on the deterioration of a body? How do you know it's not the bones of an Indian child buried before Columbus came to America?"

"I don't know," Simon said. "I'm just telling you what they found, and where they found it. It just seems like what you've been dreaming might be more than a dream."

"You know me," Lev said. "And you knew me when we were boys. Do you think I could have killed someone? Didn't you say you've had similar dreams?"

"I'm not saying," Simon said. "But maybe you should go to the police and make some inquiries. Find out what they know. They can tell you if a child went missing around that time. And lab tests will be able to determine the age, the sex, and whether it's been in the ground for hundreds of years or just sixty."

"You want me to implicate myself because I had this dream? Simon, what are you saying? I never killed anybody."

"I'm not saying you did. But wouldn't you want to know? To be sure?"

"No," Lev said. "I wouldn't. I'm okay with keeping my dreams out of my reality. How do you know it wasn't you who buried some kid there and that's why you drove by, and why you stopped? Maybe your God was trying to tell you something. Maybe it's you who have to atone."

"I'll leave now," Simon said. "Maybe you can read about it in the papers."

"Good of you to go out of your way to tell me, Rabbi," Lev said. "I'll pray those bones had nothing to do with me."

When the story appeared, it was only a paragraph on the inside page of the newspaper. But a few weeks later, there was a more detailed story. The bones had been identified as those of a boy who had gone to school with Lev and Simon. Both men recognized the name.

"What are you going to do?" Simon asked Lev after they read this report.

"I'm going to do nothing," Lev responded. "What would you like me to do?"

"Are you asking me as your friend or as a rabbi?"

"What's the difference? You've always been a rabbi, even when you were a kid."

"I think this is a great burden," Simon said. "I don't think you can just let it go. Maybe you should see a shrink or a hypnotist, try to unlock your subconscious."

"And then what? Go to prison for something I have no memory of? Just because I had a dream?"

"A recurring dream," Simon pointed out.

"I've had recurring dreams of *shtupping* Marilyn Monroe. Doesn't mean I did it."

"I'm just saying…."

"Enough of your just saying. Let's just say I never told you about my dreams, okay? Let's forget about it."

But Simon couldn't forget about it. Simon was a spiritual leader. He believed in right and wrong. He counseled ethical behavior. He couldn't live with himself covering up a murder, no matter how close he was to Lev.

"I'm going to have to say something," Simon told Lev a few days later. "I've been thinking about it. Praying for you. Asking God what is the right thing to do."

"And God told you to betray your brother?" Lev asked.

"No, God didn't tell me anything. It's what I feel inside. It's what I believe to be the right thing. You don't have to confess anything. You only have to look into yourself, with the help of a therapist. Find out what might have happened. Unlock what's been locked within you, if there is something there."

"And if I don't want to go into therapy, what are you going to do, Simon? Are you going to turn me in? A rabbi walks into a police station and says, 'I want to report a dream murder'?"

"Come to the synagogue. We'll pray together."

"You sure you want to be alone with me, Simon? If I killed once, how do you know I might not kill again?"

"I'll take my chances," Simon said.

"Okay," Lev said. "I'll see you in shul."

WHAT DREAMS MAY COME

The Last Interview with Evelyn Stardust
July 2090

World News Today *sent reporter Josh Gotoell to talk to Nobel laureate Evelyn Stardust last week, on the occasion of her 75th birthday, not knowing this would be the brilliant neuroscientist's final interview. Stardust was born July 4, 2015 in Taos, New Mexico. She went to M.I.T. at sixteen, graduated in three years, and did her doctoral work at the University of Oxford. In 2040 she received a MacArthur Genius Grant in recognition of her work in functional magnetic resonance imaging of the human brain. At John Hopkins School of Medicine, she led a team of scientists studying which parts of the brain reacted to words, faces or smell, that led to her discovery of how human thought could be captured outside an individual's mind. Her breakthrough came in 2074, when she was able to demonstrate how our tangible brains form our intangible minds. It took ten years for her research to be accepted by the scientific community and five years after that Stardust was*

awarded the Nobel Prize for her innovative work. But her find-
ings were not without controversy, as Stardust changed the way
people lived their lives and altered the nature of their dreams so
their spirit could continue peacefully throughout eternity.

Q: Ms. Stardust, how do you explain your work?
EVELYN STARDUST: Before me, no one really knew
what happened after we died. There was plenty of specula-
tion. Articles and books about the afterlife were as popular
as those dealing with aliens, UFOs, or Abraham Lincoln.
Mediums, psychics and people who shared their near-death
experiences wrote about the light at the end of a tunnel, about
being greeted by deceased loved ones and former pets, about
having been reincarnated, or atoning for one's sins, getting
one's wings, meeting our Lord and Savior or that horned
beast down under. Shakespeare came close when he had
Hamlet speak about being or not being, when he says, "To
sleep, perchance to dream—ay, there's the rub: For in that
sleep of death what dreams may come, When we have shuffled off this mortal coil..." The Bard understood that when
it came time to dying in one's sleep, what one was dreaming at the time of death could be significant. In Hamlet's
soliloquy, he speaks of "the dread of something after death,
The undiscovere'd country, from whose bourn No traveler
returns."
Q: Did you think it was possible to discover such undiscovered
country?
ES: Whatever happens after we take our final breath is undiscovered country. There is no return. As Shakespeare wrote,
it "... puzzles the will, and makes us rather bear those ills we

have Than fly to others that we know not of." The preference for staying with the known, rather than venturing into the unknown, especially when you're tampering with eternity, is what all but the bravest and adventurous preferred from the time of Adam and Eve to the time when I perfected my brain machine in the winter of 2074. It was only then that it became clear what each living person was in for when he or she passed. It wasn't what anyone had expected.

Q: *What led you into this research?*

ES: From the time I turned sixteen and had read about Marie Curie and Hedy Lamarr, I wanted to distinguish myself. The brain was still undiscovered territory in spite of the incredible technological advancements that made the last half of the 21st century so prominent. In fact, it was in the early part of the century when Functional MRIs were developed, and those brain scans gave us our first inklings of the human thought process in action. That gave a tremendous boost to cognitive neuroscience, which tried to distinguish between consciousness and free will. It was during the Trump presidency that scientists began working on preserving the knowledge and memories of individuals long after their bodies had failed. Predictions were made of the day when a detailed map of the brain, down to the neurons and synapses, would be a standard part of autopsies, making one's knowledge and experience available through analysis or simulation software after one's demise. It led to the question: If your memories and personality are somehow preserved in a computer, will this alter what it means to be dead?

Q: *Was this a question that motivated you?*

ES: Indeed. And it would take nearly a half century to uncover the answer.

Q: *How did you begin to unlock such a powerful mystery?*

ES: I began my research with monkeys and dolphins and was recognized with grants and prizes for my ability to communicate with those animals. But it was my discovery of processes in the brain just before it shuts down that led to the Nobel Prize in Physiology in 2089.

My research unlocked the mystery of brain activity when one dies in one's sleep, but not what happens when one dies in an accident, and it led to widespread fear and panic that changed the way people spent the waning months or years of their lives.

Q: *Didn't this disturb you? Did you ever worry that you were taking your research into territory that might result in so much fear and panic?*

ES: I'm a scientist, not an ethicist. By wiring and cross wiring the brains of those who allowed me to study them when death seemed imminent, I was able to not just monitor their dream states, but actually visualize onto computer monitors what these dying souls were dreaming about. What shocked the world was that these dreams continued after the person dreaming them expired. They just kept going, like a never-ending movie.

Q: *So, Shakespeare had it right when he wrote of "the dread of something after death."*

ES: He did, in part. It didn't always have to be dread. What I discovered was that when people died, their dreams lived on. If their dreams were sunny and bright, their eternity would be sunny and bright. If they were having a nightmare, they would be locked into that nightmare, on and on, horribly and infinitely.

Q: *So, you proved the existence of Heaven and Hell.*

ES: Yes. And neither had anything to do with religion or spirituality.

Q: *Which is what led to the crushing panic.*

ES: True. No one wanted their last dream to be a bad dream, because that would be Hell.

Q: *How long did it take before your research was accepted?*

ES: It took five years for my research to be corroborated, and five more before the government stepped in to set up End-of-Life Dreaming Stations, so people could find professional help learning how to dream pleasant dreams. Drugs were involved, to help ensure the bliss people sought as they bade goodbye to mortal life. To my dismay, it became a golden age for pharmaceuticals.

Q: *It also led to the Big Brother state most countries have now adopted.*

ES: For the most part, yes. But there have been outliers. Some resisted these Dream Stations because they felt them to be too Orwellian, so they practiced meditation in small groups or watched feel-good comedies or read books that made them laugh. My discovery put an end to horror films, macabre stories, PTSD documentaries, and anything to do with sadness. People just didn't want to put such images into their heads that might pop up in a dream one day. No one wanted to think about zombies, monsters, the crippled or diseased, the lonely or depressed. They preferred to focus on narrow-minded bliss.

Q: *Which kind of turned most people into end-of-life zombies.*

ES: Unfortunately, yes. My findings weren't something that could be refuted, though scientists are still trying. If it could be shown that our final dreams weren't our eternal dreams, then people could relax and accept death as what happens to everyone, and if some wanted to believe that having lived a wholesome life would be rewarded and having lived a nasty life would be punished for ever-after, then to each his own. But to know that none of that counted in the end, that it was really just a throw of the dice when it came to one's last dream, it was just too risky to leave it to chance.

Q: *Speaking of Chance....*

ES: Yes — until Chance Harcourt came along, ten years after I watched my first dying patient's last dream. Chance was a man on a mission. The world had lost its zest, he believed, because people were just too afraid to dream big dreams, to look boldly to the future, to spread their wings and soar. Life had become monotonous, robotic and boring. People smiled fake smiles, they never complained or got into fights. They just moved passively through life, knowing that true life, eternal life, began after they died, so they waited out their eighty or one hundred years on Earth so they could dream that final, grand, affirmative dream and frolic forever in what they had trained themselves for during their time being alive.

What interested Chance Harcourt wasn't the 90% of the population who spent most of their free time in Dream Stations, but those who didn't care what happened to them after they died. These were the outcasts, the rebels, the muggers and killers whose brains were wired differently than most. What the great majority saw as nightmares to avoid, they saw as excitement. They were thrilled at being chased, at committing crimes, at thinking up new ways to bleed and torture their fellow man or beast. And what Chance did was combine a little of these outsiders' DNA with a lot of the DNA of the Bored and Obedient.

Q: *And he got results, didn't he?*

ES: The result of his experiments produced humans who were not dependent on Dream Stations but willing to invest in themselves, take risks, and see Life for what it was: glorious, mysterious, challenging, and unknowable. Chance Harcourt turned scared and passive people back to being normal. That made Chance Harcourt a dangerous man in the eyes of most governments. For obvious reasons, governments preferred sheep over mustangs.

Q: *Where did you stand regarding Harcourt?*

ES: I thought Chance's formula could use some tweaking and when we met, we found that we weren't at odds, but in synch. I was not happy with the way my Final Dreams determined how people would live their lives. It concerned me; much the way Albert Einstein was concerned when he helped unleash the splitting of the atom. But once the genie was out of the bottle, I didn't know how to recap it. So, Chance's DNA elixir gave us both hope, until I realized that Chance wasn't in it for humanitarian reasons, but to profit from his genetic manipulations.

Q: *And so, you split with him?*

ES: Chance left the country, to pursue his mind-altering cocktails first in Central America, and then in Southeast Asia. While he was gone, I did more testing on his DNA concoctions and found a flaw that could not only be fatal for those who took it but could lead to dreams of disproportionate nightmares that would ruin people's afterlives. I knew it would be up to me to track down Chance and work together with him to fix the flaw. And if it couldn't be fixed, to stop him from continuing his work. One way or another.

***

Evelyn Stardust finished her interview with *World News Today* at 5:00 p.m. and went to sleep three hours later. Talking about her discovery and what had happened to the world afterwards had exhausted her. Before she slept, she put on the headgear that monitored her dreams, and she died dreaming about the interview she had given, and chasing down Chance Harcourt, wherever he might be.

***

"This is remarkable," Benjamin Stardust said, as he and his sister, Hedy, watched their mother's final dream on the monitor in her office.

"It's so much like her," Hedy said, "the literary references, the dreams about her discoveries as if she were writing her memoir, the turmoil within her, her taking a chance on Chance, the wordplay she so enjoyed, and the thrill of ending her mortal life dreaming of a purpose, of an adventure, of trying to save the world from itself."

"She will go through eternity hunting the man whose formula had the potential to do more harm than her discoveries," Benjamin said. "And because the flaw in Harcourt's formula wasn't corrected while she lived, it will never be corrected for her, in the spirit world, or dream world, or whatever dimension she entered with that last dream."

"But that doesn't matter," Hedy said. "For her, it was always the search."

"Unless by some twist of afterlife fate she manages to find him."

"Then what?" Hedy wondered.

SLEEP NO MORE

When J. awoke, he discovered that his wife had turned into a corpse.

He knew something was different when he woke first. Usually, she was the one whose feet rubbed his legs as she began her morning ritual of slowly getting out of bed. This time, he was the one who slid his foot up and down her calf. Then he turned to look at her face, her eyes closed peacefully. A face he had studied for fifty years. A face he knew like no other, including his own. And what he had seen in her eyes when she looked at him was the same love she had seen when he looked back at her.

She slept on her back and barely moved throughout the night. When she awoke, it was always with a smile. "Did you sleep?" she would ask, meaning did J. sleep well or did he get up three or four times that night? They would exchange smiles, and sometimes they would stay in bed and greet the morning by joining together. That didn't happen as often as it used to, but the night before, the last night, they had been passionate. Unusually so. Making J. think he had something to do with her not waking this morning.

He put his hand softly around her upper arm and squeezed. He leaned over her, putting his hands on her shoulders, and shook her. He put his face close to hers and whispered, "Honey, wake up."

When he got out of bed, he looked for his phone to call 911. But he hesitated. He wasn't ready for the sound of a siren, the march of medics up the stairs, the removal of the woman he loved. Instead, he went to the kitchen, boiled some water, and made himself a cup of coffee. There'd be plenty of time to mourn, to bury, to sleep alone.

He was surprised at how calm he was. This was the moment he had dreaded more than any other. He had suffered when each of his parents passed, had sobbed in great gulps when his best friend succumbed, but his love for them paled compared to the love he had for his wife. She was his partner in life. They had shared everything, the sorrows and the joys, the secrets that only they knew. He had lost a part of himself, the best part, and yet he was able to make his coffee and sit in the living room, looking out the window at the sky. The blue sky, the white clouds, the warm morning. He was by himself, but as long as she was still in the house he didn't feel alone.

"You okay?"

He looked up. She was standing ten feet away from him.

"You didn't make me coffee?" she asked.

"You didn't wake up," he said, his eyes blinking rapidly, as if they were small slaps that would shake him back to reality.

"I think maybe we overdid it last night," she said, smiling. "I was like dead."

"Like dead? You mean …. you're not dead?"

"What are you talking about? Why should I be dead? You were strong, but you didn't kill me."

"Oh my God, K. Oh my God!"

He stood and spilled the coffee on the floor.

"What's wrong with you?" she asked. "You look pale."

"If you're a ghost, then I should be pale. If it's you, then I'm just an idiot. I thought you had died. I pinched you, I shook you, I stood over you. You didn't move. I couldn't feel your breath."

"And then you came in here and brewed coffee? You didn't call 911?"

"I was going to. But not yet. I wanted more time with you."

"What were you going to do with that time?"

"Just to know you were still here. I needed time to think."

"How come you weren't crying?"

"I know, isn't that something? You'd think I'd be a wreck. But it was like, you were so at peace, we had made such good love, it was a good way to go, if you had to go."

"So, you were celebrating? Drinking coffee. Listening to the birds."

"Didn't hear the birds. I'm just so relieved. I can't believe it. How could I have been so stupid, to think you were dead when you were just in a deep sleep." And then J. began to cry. It was tears that were the opposite of grief. K. was back. She had never left. Their lives would go on, together, for who knows how long? It was all he wanted.

K. went back to their bedroom and J. followed. She was there, in bed, on her back. She looked so peaceful with her eyes closed. He spoke to her, but she didn't answer. But that was all right.

He was glad he had waited.

CHEATERS

SHOES

From: service3 <customer.services@customerser-vicebest.com>

To: S. Hasseldorf <shasseldorf@gmail.com>

Sent: Tuesday, May 19, 2020, 12:30:34 AM PDT

Subject: [TID:1616163] Order Information, Payment No.PS2005190320434813

Dear customer,

CONGRATULATIONS ON YOUR SUCCESSFUL PURCHASE OF OUR ULTRA-LOW-COST LIMITED PROMOTIONAL PRODUCTS!

Product: *ECCO Mens Cage Pro,1,24.00, ECCO Mens Soft 7 Low GTX,1,20.00, ECCO Womens BIOM Venture GTX,1,20.00, ECCO Womens Yucatan Sandal,1,19.00.*

Total Amount: *USD 83.0.*

Delivery Address: S. Hasseldorf, *P.O. Box 3118, Duluth, MN 55802*

It will take a few days for our related department to process your order, we will email you the tracking number when the order is shipped out. Please wait be patient!

If you have any problems, please feel free to contact us.

Have a nice day!
Best Regards,
Customer Service Department

Dear Service3,
Glad to hear that my order has been successful.
However, I was wondering if it would be possible
to change one of the shoe orders for something
else? I would prefer to order two pairs of the golf
shoes, and eliminate the men's walking shoe.
S. Hasseldorf

From: service3 <customer.services@customerser-vicebest.com>
To: S. Hasseldorf <shasseldorf@gmail.com>
Sent: Wednesday, May 20, 2020, 05:50:57 PM PDT
Subject: [TID:1616163] Order Information, Payment No.PS2005190320434813
Dear customer,
We have changed that for you, please don't worry.
Any problem please feel free to contact us.
Have a good day.
Regards!

Dear Service3,
I am not worried. Thank you for making the
change. I look forward to the shoes.
S. Hasseldorf

From: service3 <customer.services@customerser-vicebest.com>
To: S. Hasseldorf <shasseldorf@gmail.com>
Sent: Thursday, May 21, 2020, 06:41:18 PM PDT
Subject: [TID:1616163] Order Information, Payment No.PS2005190320434813
Dear customer,
Thanks for your understand and kindness.
Have a good day.
Regards!

Dear Service3,
Not sure what you mean by my understanding and kindness when, in fact, it was you who was understanding about my asking to make a change in my order and it was you who was kind to allow it. So, thank you for your understanding and kindness.
S. Hasseldorf

From: service3 <customer.services@customerser-vicebest.com>
To: S. Hasseldorf <shasseldorf@gmail.com>
Sent: Saturday, May 23, 2020, 04:41:19 AM PDT
Subject: [TID:1616163] Your Tracking Number RV436900673CN for your goods., Order No.PS2005190320434813
Dear customer,
Thanks for your patience.

We have sent your order via China Post or China Post EMS, but the certain shipping time depends on the different countries.

The tracking No. is: RV436900673CN

Please check the status through the link:

https://t.17track.net/en#nums=RV436900673CN

Please wait patiently, too.

Please kindly check your spam box, because the related mails may be there.

Best regards!

Dear Service3,

Very glad to hear that the order has been shipped so quickly. Of course, I understand that the shipping may take a while and I will patiently wait for their arrival.

S. Hasseldorf

From: service3 <customer.services@customerservicebest.com>

To: S. Hasseldorf <shasseldorf@gmail.com>

Sent: Sunday, May 24, 2020, 10:38:27 PM PDT

Subject: [TID:1616163] Order Information, Payment No.PS2005190320434813

Dear customer,

Thanks for your patient.

We have shipped the order by EMS, the tracking No. is RV436900673CN.

You can contact with us if you have any problem.

Best regards,

Dear Service3,

Once again, my compliments for keeping me so well informed and providing the tracking number for the four pairs of shoes I ordered. From your quick responses, I do not expect to have any problems.

Sincerely,

S. Hasseldorf

From: service3 <customer.services@customerservicebest.com>

To: S. Hasseldorf <shasseldorf@gmail.com>

Sent: Tuesday, May 26, 2020, 11:44:55 PM PDT

Subject: [TID:1616163] Order Information, Payment No.PS2005190320434813:

Dear customer,

If there are problems, don't worry.

Regards!

Dear Service3,

Well, it seems that there is a problem, after all. Today I received from China a small package of ten cotton face masks. As I have not ordered anything other than shoes from China, I wonder if you sent these, and if you did, why?

S. Hasseldorf

From: service3 <customer.services@customerservicebest.com>

To: S. Hasseldorf <shasseldorf@gmail.com>

Sent: Thursday, June 18, 2020, 11:44:55 PM PDT
Subject: [TID:1616163] Order Information, Payment No.PS2005190320434813
Dear customer
Sorry for the trouble.
Could you please send us the picture of the item you received and also the picture of the package with label? Only you send us the pictures, can we investigate that for you and solve the problem for you.
Hope you can understand that and looking forward to your reply.
Regards,

Dear Service3,
Not sure why you need a picture of the face masks, but am attaching, along with the envelope it came in. S. Hasseldorf

From: service3 <customer.services@customerservicebest.com>
To: S. Hasseldorf <shasseldorf@gmail.com>
Sent: Friday, June 19, 2020, 11:02:37 PM PDT
Subject: [TID:1616163] Order Information, Payment No.PS2005190320434813
Dear customer,
Really sorry for that.
We have investigated that for you, but as there are too many packages in the process of logistics and transportation, the express company mixed your parcel with others.

Do you need to exchange the wrong package?
Looking for your reply.
Sincerely!

Dear Service3,
No, I do not need to exchange the wrong package.
I just would like to receive the right package: four
pairs of shoes that I ordered and paid for.
S. Hasseldorf

From: service3 <customer.services@customerser-
vicebest.com>
To: S. Hasseldorf <shasseldorf@gmail.com>
Sent: Sunday, June 21, 2020, 07:56:37 PM PDT
Subject: [TID:1616163] Order Information, Payment
No.PS2005190320434813
Dear customer,
Sorry for that we checked our warehouse and found
that the item you ordered is out of stock due to previ-
ous product promotion.
You can log in the link to browse our existing
products
https://www.fashiononlinemall.com/index/
login/quicklogin.html?email=shasseldorf@gmail.
com&oid=PS2005190320434813
And if there is some one you like, you can add that
to the wish list or send us the picture, and then tell
us you have chose something.
Looking forward your reply
Regards!

Dear Service3,

I do not have a wish list, other than just a wish to receive what I ordered or else get a refund for that order. I looked at the link you sent and do not see anything there that I want.

S. Hasseldorf

From: service3 <customer.services@customerservicebest.com>
To: S. Hasseldorf <shasseldorf@gmail.com>
Sent: Monday, June 22, 2020, 06:46:58 PM PDT
Subject: [TID:1616163] Order Information, Payment No.PS2005190320434813

Dear customer,

Sorry for the trouble.

In order to solve this problem:

1, You could keep the item you received, as a gift for your family or friend, and we could refund you 38% of your order's value.

2, You could return it and pay the return-shipping fee by yourself, we will give you full refund after receiving the return package.

Looking forward to your reply.

Sincerely,

Dear Service3,

In my country, a gift is something given without an expectation of payment. If one pays for a gift, it is no longer considered a gift, but a purchase. I did not order the face masks that I received. To be

honest, since they have come from your country, and that is also where the virus has come from, it would be foolish of me to think of using them. It would be best to dispose of them. I don't see the point of spending more money to ship them back to you, where it would be wrong to repackage and resell, or re-"gift" them to anyone else. I don't know where you came up with the figure of 38% as a fair refund, but I find that unacceptable.
S. Hasseldorf

From: service3 <customer.services@customerservicebest.com>
To: S. Hasseldorf <shasseldorf@gmail.com>
Sent: Tuesday, June 23, 2020, 08:05:02 PM PDT
Subject: [TID:1616163] Order Information, Payment No.PS2005190320434813
Dear customer,
As there is no freight insurance, so if you return the package, you need pay it by yourself.
We don't want to bother you so much, hope you can reconsider our 38% refund and keep the item you received.
Looking forward your reply.
Regards!

Dear Service3,
As previously stated, I don't think it wise or prudent to send cheap cotton face masks back and forth between China and the U.S. Nor do I intend

to keep them myself. They will be disposed of. As for reconsidering your very ungenerous offer, the answer is no, I will not reconsider it. I would like to be treated fairly. If you want to deduct the cost of those face masks, then take the two dollars they are worth. If you want to deduct the shipping cost as well, then take another five dollars. In other words, please refund me 90% of the money I sent you.
S. Hasseldorf

From: service3 <customer.services@customerser-vicebest.com>
To: S. Hasseldorf <shasseldorf@gmail.com>
Sent: Sunday, June 28, 2020, 12:01:09 AM PDT
Subject: [TID:1616163] Order Information, Payment No.PS2005190320434813
Dear customer,
We also want to solve this case for you.
But hope you can understand that we also had lost much on this transaction, shipping fee, product, manual cost ....
It is difficult for us to apply full refund for you.
How about we give you 43% of the order's value, then let's finish this issue?
We don't want to bother you so much.
Regards!

Dear Service3,
Let us look at this developing situation. On May 19, I received notice from you about my "successful

purchase," listing the names of the 4 pairs of shoes I ordered. The following day, I wrote to say that I wanted to change one of those pairs of shoes to another style and you said you made the change and told me not to worry. Three days later you emailed me to say the shipment had gone out. But then, when I wrote to tell you that I received a small package of cotton face masks from China, you asked me to send you a photo of the package. Once you got the photo, you came to the conclusion that the wrong package was sent. Obviously, a small envelope of face masks does not equal 4 large boxes of shoes. When I asked you to send me the correct order, the one that I had already paid for, you told me what I ordered was "out of stock." So, obviously, you NEVER completed the order in the first place, as you had told me on May 23. And then you had the audacity to ask me to return the face masks (which I would have to pay to return) for a refund of what I paid you, or you would refund me 38% of what I paid. When I questioned the logic of this, you upped your offer by 5% (to 43%) asking me to "understand that we also had lost much on this transaction, shipping fee, product, manual cost...."

So, here's my response:

1) I DO NOT understand that you have "lost much on this transaction." I paid you $87.50 for SHOES. You sent me some face masks,

of very little value, at very little cost. I might understand the "manual cost" of someone in a warehouse finding the correct shoes to send; but there is miniscule manual cost for selecting and sending the wrong product of a handful of face masks.

2) Had I ordered the face masks and they were the wrong size, then I would understand needing to return them. But these are face masks, they are not reusable after they go back and forth through the mails from China to the U.S and back to China. They are disposable and should be thrown away. So, it makes no sense to spend money to return something that was NEVER ordered. This is a mistake on YOUR part, and it is up to you to correct your mistake.

3) It is clear to me that you do not tell the truth, indicated by your telling me a) that you made the change to one of the pairs I had ordered and b) that you shipped them out, because c) you then said you never had the shoes in the first place since they were "out of stock."

4) Since I am keeping track of all this, I will eventually notify the authorities in your country, as well as my own, unless this issue is correctly resolved and the only way to resolve this is to refund my money. I've indicated that I would allow a 10% deduction from the purchase price to cover whatever minor expenses this has created, even though

none of these expenses are due to my errors. This is all on you, and if you want to truly resolve this honestly, then you will do the right thing.

Sincerely hoping you will acknowledge the error of your ways,
S. Hasseldorf

From: service3 <customer.services@customerservicebest.com>
To: S. Hasseldorf <shasseldorf@gmail.com>
Sent: Sunday, June 28, 2020, 08:20:50 PM PDT
Subject: [TID:1616163] Order Information, Payment No.PS2005190320434813
Dear customer,
Sorry for this case.
According to the policy, if you want a full refund, you should return the item you received and pay the return-shipping fee by yourself. After we receive the return package, we will arrange the refund to you.
Considering your benefit, we still recommend you to keep the item you received and we can apply 45% refund for you.
Looking forward your reply
Regards!

Dear President Xi JinPing
Zhongnanhai Fuyou Street Branch P.O.

I would like to alert you that there is a company in China that represents itself as reputable when, in fact, it is anything but. They advertise on Facebook and probably other American social media outlets, offering what appears to be great deals, brand name shoes in my case, and then after they receive an order and are paid for the items, they do not fulfill their side of the bargain. In other words, they cheat. They also lie, as I have discovered through a series of emails. They are a fraudulent outfit, for all I know maybe even a single person, doing to the American consumer what the Russian hackers did to the Democratic nominee for president in 2016, and most likely will do again in 2020 and 2024. As someone who has followed how China works, I cannot assume that you would allow such shenanigans to go on under your nose. We in America know that you have tremendous control over your citizens. I am calling this company and/or citizen out and hope that you do the right thing and imprison them.

Sincerely,

S. Hasseldorf

Dear Service3,

This is to notify you that your days are numbered. I have, through channels of my own, informed your president of your deceit. You thought you could hide behind your email address and never signing off after each email. Well, think again, because you can't pull the wool over my eyes, even though you think that because I am an American you can get away with anything. Well, to this I say, Ha! And I will say it again, Ha! If you'd like to refund my money now, well, too late. Am not sorry about that! S. Hasseldorf

From: Office of President Xi JinPing, Zhongnanhai Fuyou Street Branch P.O.
To: S. Hasseldorf <shasseldorf@gmail.com>
Sent: Sat, July 4, 2020, 12:000 PM PDT
Subject: [TID:1616163] Order Information, Payment No.PS2005190320434813

Dear S. Hasseldorf,

We have looked into this matter between you and Service3. We are sorry you feel that you have been a victim of fraud and deceit. However, from what we were able to discern, the company acted in good faith and tried, with each of their responses to you, to make you a satisfied customer. The fact that they sent you face masks instead of shoes indicates that they were substituting your welfare over your comfort. For that, we commend them and will be sending them a Certificate of Commendation. As for your political references, it is our policy to stay out of your country's politics, though we notice that today is your Independence Day and we wish you a happy day of fireworks and hot dogs. That Service3 is offering you a return of 45% of your money, we feel that is a very generous offer. You should take it.

Assistant to the Personnel Officer
Office of President Xi JinPing

Dear Service3
July 5, 2020
I have decided that rather than accept your offer to refund me 45% of my money because you didn't send me the shoes I ordered, I have looked again at the link you sent of your existing products, and will accept these 4 pairs of shoes:

1. SKMOD 1000 494
2. SKMOD 1000 499
3. SKMOD 1000 548
4. SKMOD 1000 183

The size for all 4 pairs is 10.5

Please let me know when I can expect them

Thank you,
S. Hasseldorf

On Wednesday, July 6, 2020, 10:25:26 PM PDT, service3 <customer.services@customerservicebest.com> wrote:

Thank you for changing your mind. We too have changed ours. The shoes are no longer available. The refund is also unavailable. We hope you make good use of the masks.
Regards!

ALL MY BOGEYS SHOULD HAVE BEEN PARS

Among the people on the guest list for the January 2005 wedding between Donald Trump and the Slovenian beauty Melania Knauss were former president Bill Clinton and his wife, Senator Hillary Clinton. Before the big event at Trump's Mar-A-Lago, Donald and Bill snuck off for a quick round of golf, a game better described by their caddies as One-Upmanship.

Clinton hadn't brought his clubs with him on the flight to West Palm Beach and Trump generously loaned him a bag of second-hand Callaways. "Shot my third hole-in-one with that 3-wood," Trump told Clinton.

"How many have you had since then?" Clinton asked.

"Just two," Trump said. "But five's a pretty good number, wouldn't you say?"

"Sure-as-shit is," the former president drawled. "And I bet four of them were made when you played alone."

"I never play alone," Trump smiled. "If I did, no one would believe how good I am. I've won the club championship at each of my clubs."

Clinton had heard that when Trump opened a new club, he played the first round with just his caddy, then called it a championship, so his name would go up on the board. "And I secretly put a man on Mars," Clinton said.

"Now, that's a secret worth knowing," Trump said.

Clinton smiled and shook his head. "These clubs might have lost their juice after you used them so well," he said.

"Tell you what, Bill. Why don't you use my clubs, top of the line TaylorMades, and I'll use the Callaways. Maybe we can make it interesting."

"What's your game?" asked Clinton

"Five hundred a hole?" Trump suggested.

"Bit shallow for the two of us, wouldn't you say? Since this is your club, and your course, and I haven't played much golf lately, how about you give me three holes, and we'll make it five thousand a hole, just for laughs."

"Why don't I give you four holes, and we'll make it ten."

"Now you're talking," Clinton laughed. "Hillary wasn't sure about coming, but I knew we'd have some fun down here."

With Trump down forty-grand before either of them swung a club, Clinton was all smiles. So was Donald. He hadn't played with Clinton before, but he heard he was a duffer, and he thought he could make up those holes by the time they reached the sixth tee.

On the first hole, Trump gave Clinton the honors and Clinton hooked his ball into the left rough. "First hole jitters," Trump said as he teed up his ball and put his full weight into his drive. The ball bounced twice down the fairway and then buried itself in a sand trap.

"That trap's 260 yards away," Trump said. "Guess I'll have to take it down a bit."

Clinton managed to get out of the rough and onto the green in three more strokes; Trump took two shots to get out of the sand, and both men wound up with double bogeys.

"That's one less hole for you to catch up," Clinton said, recalling a joke about a priest and a rabbi playing golf for the first time. Trump didn't catch the punchline but asked the former president why golf was better than sex. Clinton said he didn't know it was. Trump said, "You can stop half-way through for a burger and fries, and it doesn't affect your performance."

As they played, the two horndogs began comparing notes on the women they had grabbed, and how their fame allowed them to get away with such despicable behavior. Trump wasn't impressed with some of the young women that got Clinton impeached, but what did pique his curiosity was how he kept Hillary from leaving him. "Must have cost you a pretty penny," he said before Clinton putted for a birdie.

"Wasn't about money, Donald," Clinton said as he sank the putt. "Just politics."

"Mine have always given me leeway, until things jumped from Page Six to the Front Page. I probably cover a year's rent for Cartier's each time," Trump smirked.

"You still dabbing other inkwells or you going to settle down with Melania?"

"She's a beauty, isn't she? But it's tough to keep it in my pants when it's all out there for the taking."

"Don't I know it," Clinton laughed.

They both exaggerated their stories of conquest and divide and conquer, taking the same kind of liberties with their memories as they did with their golf games. Neither man felt shame by moving a golf ball out of a bad lie or dropping a replacement instead of admitting to a lost ball. Golf was a game of honor, now being played for high stakes by dishonorable men. But since both men took liberties, it was just a matter of who was the better cheater that would determine the outcome of their match.

By the tenth hole, Trump had won three holes, Clinton had won two, and they squared the other four, which meant Trump was down $30,000. Clinton was enjoying himself more than his host, who wolfed down two hamburgers and a root beer before teeing off on the back nine. Clinton preferred peanut butter and pineapple sandwiches and a real beer.

On the par five tenth hole, Trump was on the green in three and three-putted. Clinton also bogeyed the hole. With eight holes to go and still down $30,000, Trump stopped joking and began jabbing at Clinton's poor taste in women, and how history would not be kind to his shenanigans while in office. But Clinton was used to such barbs and didn't rattle. He suppressed a chuckle when Trump missed a three-footer that turned a par into another bogey on the twelfth, and again on the thirteenth.

"These fucking bogeys should have been pars," Trump grumbled. "They were actually gimmees."

"You're only down four holes, Donald, with five to play. Want to double up these last five?"

"Tell you what, Bill. Why don't we double the next two, then double that for the last three?"

"With those stakes," Clinton said, "maybe you'd like your clubs back."

"I win the next two holes, we're even," Trump said. "I win the three after, I'm up $120,000."

Trump managed to win the next hole and they squared the fifteenth. With Clinton still up $20,000, Trump drove his ball into the trees on the sixteenth. Clinton played it safe with a hybrid off the tee and kept his shot in the fairway. When Trump's caddy found his ball, it was buried behind an oak tree. The caddy kicked it to a better position, and Trump used his three iron to move the ball again, giving himself a clear opening to the green. Clinton and his caddy were far enough away not to see this, but Clinton assumed Trump would give himself every advantage on these final holes. He sliced his second shot into a trap on the right side of the green and watched as Trump hit his second shot onto the fringe. Clinton's third shot cleared the bunker but left him thirty feet from the pin. Trump putted his third to within three feet of the cup. "This a gimmee?" he asked the former president.

"Let's see what I do with this first," Clinton said, stroking his ball next to Trump's marker. "Guess we'll both have to putt out," he said.

Clinton knocked his in for a par; Trump's ball rimmed the cup and stayed out. "Another fucking bogey that should have been a par," he muttered.

"No sweat, Donald. You're only down sixty. Win the next two and you'll be up twenty."

"Better believe it," Trump said.

Trump had to surreptitiously move his next drive out of the rough but hit his second shot into mud by the side of a lake. He made sure Clinton didn't see him replace the muddy ball with a new one and managed to bogey the hole. Clinton missed his bogey putt bringing his advantage down to $20,000 with one hole to go.

The eighteenth was Trump's favorite hole. It was a par five that he had birdied more often than parred. How legitimate those birdies were no one would ever know, but Trump felt confident enough to propose they play the hole for a clean hundred thousand. If Clinton won, he'd get the additional twenty he was up. If Trump won, Clinton would owe him eighty.

As they drove to the last hole, Trump asked Clinton how long Hillary held out after she realized he had lied to her about Monica Lewinsky. "I bet you didn't fuck her for months," Trump said.

"You'd lose that bet," Clinton said. "I hadn't fucked her for years."

"No blow jobs?"

"I thought we were talking sex," Clinton said.

"Tell you what, how'd you like to fuck Melania on our wedding night? You win this next hole, instead of the money, you can poke my wife. Your choice."

"Well, that's mighty generous of you, Donald," Clinton said. "Can I decide when we've finished?"

"Sure, pal," Donald said. "But don't you think you should reciprocate? If I win?"

"You want to fuck Hillary?" Clinton said and started to laugh.

Trump didn't laugh, but he also didn't win. Clinton parred the eighteenth. Trump didn't, missing another three-footer that Clinton insisted he putt.

"So," Trump said through gritted teeth, "what's it gonna be? The money or my new wife?"

"You know what, Donald. Let's get back to the hotel. I'll let Hillary decide."

CHEATING

God was a trickster. Had to be. Once His little experiment with Adam and Eve got out of hand, and humans began to populate the Earth like rabbits, God realized that to keep Heaven manageable He would have to find a way to be selective.

The one deal He made with His evil adversary relieved Him of the task of having to judge all the really bad people. The murderers, rapists, embezzlers, abusers, hard drug dealers who sold to teenagers, fans of romance novels, Scientologists, Jews for Jesus, the writers of the last TV episode of *Game of Thrones*, and those who voted twice for Richard Nixon, Ronald Reagan, George W. Bush and Donald Trump would all go directly to Hell.

But that still left 30 or 40% of dead people that needed to be judged —accepted into Heaven, left dangling in Limbo, or atoning in Purgatory. So, God had to come up with ways to judge those whose souls came knocking.

One of His ways was to reject those who had never read at least one book by any of the following authors: Mark Twain, Herman Melville, Gustave Flaubert, Gabriel Garcia Marquez, Marcel Proust, James Joyce, Wole Soyinka, Chinua Achebe, Charles Dickens, Miguel de Cervantes, Leo Tolstoy, Fyodor Dostoyevsky, Toni Morrison, Ba Jin, Yasunari

Kawabata, Murasaki Shikibu, Thomas Bernhard, Lewis Carroll, or Theodore Geisel.

Another way was to keep list makers out because they drove Him crazy.

He considered eliminating those who liked cheaply made ice cream, white bread, cauliflower, or sugary breakfast cereals, but though that would certainly reduce Heaven's population by at least two-thirds, it was just too easy a solution. God preferred challenging Himself. And that's when He came up with addressing those who cheated playing Words with Friends.

It was a good word game that brought strangers together via the Internet, but then the apps came along that allowed players to type in their letters and out would spill words that could be used, like *qoph, oicks, zoril,* or *crozes.* And, even more egregious, if a question mark was typed in, a great many more words were shown. What God didn't like were cheaters. He occasionally looked down upon board game players and when He saw how people got away with cheating at Monopoly, Clue, Go or chess, it just bugged the Heaven out of Him. He put cheaters right up there with those who drew a line on a blank paper or canvas and tossed it away, or those who felt they needed to stuff their mouths with chewing gum when one piece was sufficient.

Imagine their surprise when all those newly dead came to get their wings and were told, "Sorry, but you cheated playing Words with Friends, so you're going to Hell."

"Wait, wait," these poor souls would protest. "Why Hell? Why not, at least, Limbo? Why not allow for penance? It was just a game."

Ah, they'd be told, it wasn't just a game. It was a *test*. Before the apps, it was a game. After the apps, it was an invitation to temptation. And we all know that God used temptation as a way of judging. Just look back at the Beginning. Had those two left the apple alone, there would have been no death and no clothes. Everyone would have been happy walking around naked, living forever, and God wouldn't have to spend so much time figuring out who got into Heaven or who had to be sent to Hell after they died.

"But everybody cheated on Words with Friends," everybody who cheated said, trying to convince Peter, Paul, or Mary to let them squeeze by.

"Not Bob Dylan," they were told.

"Bob Dylan played Words with Friends?" came the chorus of responses.

"Rarely lost a game," they were told.

"Impossible," came the chorus. "No one could win against a cheater."

"And no one could have written '*Blowin' in the Wind*' or '*A Hard Rain's A-Gonna Fall*,' had they dared cheat on a simple word game."

It was useless to argue with an angel, much less try to change a decree issued by the Big Guy Himself. But argue they did, each and every Heavenly reject. Had they only known, they thought retrospectively, they would never have cheated. They would never have even *played* Words with Friends. They would have stuck with Scrabble.

"Too late," they were told.

But all was not lost. Because what they were each about to find out was that the Devil loved to play Words with Friends. And since the only one allowed to use the cheating app in Hell was Satan, what the newly initiated discovered was that eternity was for losers.

STEELING

Wut I done was not hard. Pretty easy, akchully. But then I shudda known it cudnt last and that being careless wud get me caut. Serves me right, being outsmarted lik that. That Amazon guy is the richest guy in the world, so why dint I think that he would hire dicks to follo their trucks?

For a wile tho, I was getting away with it. Just follod a truck, watched where they delevered the boxes, grab the ones ware there was no cameras. Every day I follod a diffrent truck on a different root. Wore the face mask, a diffrent cap every other day, dark glasses, no one cud reconize me. Put me in a lineup and they'd have to let me go. That's why I never got a tatoo where it mite show up.

But I dint think the truck I follod had a dick behind, folloing me. Caut me red-handed. "Drop the box," is wut he sed. I tried to run, but ware was I going to go? My car was rite there. So, I tried to throw it at him, but he just stept back. The box fell by his feet. And since he was carrying, wut could I do? Let him shoot me for a box?

So now Im in this place and taking a riting class. The teacher says he's a riter and we should rite about wut got us here. Wut good will that do? I dont know. But better than sitting in my cell staring at the toylet.

So, that's wut got me here. I got caut steeling from Amazon. Big deal. Who gets hurt? People say they dint get wut they ordered, they get another shipment. Amazon got enuf to not miss wut Im taking. This really worth putting me in jail and expozing me to that virus? Shud I have to get sick and die because I took a few boxes from some peoples drivwaze?

I never knew wut I was taking. Sometimes, some pretty good stuff. An iPhone, a gambox, a nise watch, some tools. A lot of books that I just tost. Dont care much for reeding. A lot of those Kindles, some fitbits, laptops, printers, wutever. That's the stuff you can get half price for if the buyer wants it for himself, or a third of the price if he's selling it. It's not lik I was peddling dope or pain pills. And it was always a surprise, wut was in the boxes.

I never took something that cudnt fit into my trunk. Dint want some passing cop to look into the backseat and see some of the boxes. I was carful about that. But not carful enuf, as you can see. Now Im here and all of a sudden, Im a riter. Ha! My dad would get a kick out of that. Hes the one who showed me how to do this. Hes serving time now, too, but not for steeling boxes. That's another story. Im not telling that one.

Some of the guys here seem pretty nise. Even some gards, but not all. This is my first time loked up and it suks. I never been one to lik being told wut to do and wen to do it and wut not to do. I just dont want to run into some guys who want me to suk them off. Just not my thing. I hurd that happens but so far so good. A cuple of gards keep eyeing me, so I figger they might force me, but Im trying to stay away from truble, just keep it on the low, you know? Probly shud have kept some of those books, not that Im much of a reeder, but plenty of down time here. Who knows, maybe it's a good thing I got caut. Dint have much of an educashon. Dont know that many words. My spelling is for shit but that's ok, whos gonna read this anyway, exept the teacher, and wuts he gonna do with it?

Im supose to fill up a bunch of pages in this notebook they give me but wut else am I supose to say? My moms a trucker and wont find out Im here until she gets back from across the cuntry. She wont be plezed, having her old man and her son both in the slammer. But she knew I was taking boxes because a lot of the stuff I gave her. The women stuff. A lot of clothes, makup, all kinds of shit. She dont reed eether so no sense giving her the books. She's had it pretty tuff but she's pretty tuff herself. She once told me I was a mistak. Guess the old mans condum had a hole in it. But I never rezented that she told me. Im gessing most people come from mistaks. So many goddam people in the world. This virus is probly Gods way of thinning the herd. Happens all the time acording to history. This is our time. And maybe its my time and my dads time, seeing as how were locked up and all. I dout very much that theyd take us to any hospital to put us on one of those ventilaters.

Frum wut I heard they use us wen theres a big fire sumware or wen the rodes need cleaning. Thats ok if it gets us out for a wile, tho its probly danjrus and thats why they use prizners. I wunder how many excap fires?

I gess Im not supose to say that Id probly go back to steeling boxes, so I wont say that. Not saying one way or the other.

Wut I will say is that wutever I do wen I get out will be better thawt out than wut got me here. If Im supose to learn a lesson from all this its that I have to think more before I act. I have to be more carful. I have to have a plan and a backup plan. I think thats wut I can probly learn whil Im here. Im already learning to be a riter. So why shunt I learn how to be a better theef?

The End

TAKE NOTICE

I t breaks my heart to send this news, but Julie didn't wake up today. For all of you who knew and loved her, I know this will come as a shock. It certainly was to me. She wasn't ill. She wasn't suffering from anything. We ate her classic chicken dumplings and sushi rice the night before. She even drank half a beer, which, for her, was all she could handle.

I'm wracking my brain trying to get a handle on this. I'm trying to go over her last day, but nothing unusual pops up. It started around seven a.m., when NPR came on. We always let the news wake us. If it's bad news, we don't listen and sleep through it. If it's good news, well, when is the news ever good these days? Yesterday, the stock market went down, the virus numbers went up, the wildfires spread throughout the West Coast, the police shot and killed a handcuffed man, and a vigilante popped a couple of bullets into a police van, wounding two officers. Nothing out of the ordinary for a September morning.

Before breakfast, Julie did her yoga. Then she took a shower. She did something different in the shower—she shaved her pubic hair for the first time—but I think she did that to surprise me, because she came out smiling, with the towel wrapped around her, and then she casually dropped the towel and spread her arms out, as if to say, "Ta da." In fact, she did say "Ta da," and I reacted by immediately taking her back to bed. In all the years we've been together (and forgive me for being so explicit) I never licked such a smooth mons pubis. I even rubbed my cheek on it. It was, as you might imagine, very exciting.

I would never reveal such an intimate thing as this but for the fact that Julie didn't wake up this morning. So, I'm laying out the details as I can recall them, and maybe it will make sense when I'm done.

I made hot cereal for breakfast and she cut up the strawberries and banana, washed the blueberries, and crushed the walnuts. The grain I chose was steel cut oats, though I could have gone with Scottish or Irish oats, corn meal, Wheatena, buckwheat, or milled rice. Julie ground the Jamaican coffee beans and made two cups with one paper filter. Most mornings we also have a green juice smoothie, but we skipped it yesterday. We did take our blood pressure and cholesterol pills, and all the daily vitamins and supplements we've been swallowing for years.

The night wind sent down the usual shower of leaves from the trees, so after breakfast I raked the lawn and swept the patio while Julie cleaned the pine needles from the garden. Then she went inside to empty the dryer, changed the bed sheets, got comfortable on the couch and started reading Bob Woodward's new book. I went to my office to clean my desk, which is an impossible task. Because the air quality was "unacceptable," we refrained from taking a walk outside, but Julie did three miles on the treadmill, worked up a sweat, and took a shower afterwards.

Midday, she made ramen for lunch and we ate it while watching MSNBC. It was the same old same old, so we started watching a documentary I had taped about a wild octopus that befriended a man. Julie was impressed with how intelligent the octopus was but said she would still eat them raw whenever we went to our favorite Japanese restaurants. "But with greater respect," she joked.

We only watched half the documentary, and then Julie went to her office to work on her novel about a woman who had two families, neither of which knew anything about the other. I'm not sure how long she wrote, but I know she took a break to meditate for twenty minutes. It always refreshed her.

We did have a small argument around this time because I started vacuuming while she was deep into her concentration. She asked me to stop, but I was dealing with the spider webs on the walls and steps near her office and wanted to finish what I was doing. I don't kill the spiders but empty out the vacuum container in the trash cans because that's how Julie preferred it. "You made me lose my thought," she said. I apologized but told her I didn't kill any of the spiders. "Not the point," she said.

Now, I know what you might be thinking. That I upset Julie, and because she had an arrhythmic heartbeat, this could have triggered palpitations, anxiety or stress. I don't deny this, but really, sucking up cobwebs and spiders wasn't exactly jackhammering a swimming pool, which is what our neighbors were doing all week long, from early morning until sundown. Come to think of it, the cement and granite dust from that endeavor might have entered our lungs when we were outside gardening each morning. Just saying.

I offered Julie a hybrid gummy to change her mood, but she said she still wanted to read after her meditation and the edible would be too distracting. So, I chewed a few and went about my business, whatever that might have been, as I don't remember the first two hours after the gummies took effect. That's probably when I cleaned the bathtub and the toilets because I noticed how clean they were the next day.

I do remember that we ordered in dinner from our favorite Brazilian restaurant and after we ate the lemon chicken, yucca, rice and beans, and fried plantain we thought it might be fun to have early-evening sex, which we did. And which it was. Her mons pubis was a real turn-on and I couldn't get over that, for all the years that I buried my face in her wild, fluffy pubic hair, I would feel this way about her new Chihuahua look.

Afterwards, we took a catnap, maybe thirty minutes, and then went downstairs to finish watching the octopus documentary. It ended sadly, with the poor thing being eaten by a pajama shark. But that's life in the wild. And life in captivity, too, I guess. Life is that way, isn't it? You go along your business, you make a new friend, you fall in love, you run from predators, and then your luck runs out and you die. What can you do?

What could Julie have done?

This is what I know she did. She was inspired by what we watched and when I went to bed last night, she stayed up to work on her novel. She saw something about the interaction between the diver and the cephalopod that inspired her. And this morning, when I awoke, she was still at her desk.

"How many pages?" I asked.

"Don't know," she said. "Two new chapters."

And that's why Julie didn't wake up today. She never went to sleep.

So, join us next Saturday, 8:00 p.m. at our home, to surprise Julie on her fiftieth birthday. She'll be so happy to see you all.

BELIEVERS

MAGNIFIED

Brian couldn't grasp what a virus was. His dad said it was invisible, but his mom corrected him. "Not invisible," she said, "it's microscopic." But that didn't put a picture in his mind.

"It's just very, very tiny," she explained. "So tiny that if you put the virus on your thumbnail, do you know how many there would be? Millions. Millions and millions."

But what was such a number to a five-year-old?

His dad tried to compare a virus to atoms, but that was too confusing. He tried again, with particles of dust.

"You can't see dust, but dust is right in front of you, and behind you, it's in the air. If you shine a light and look through a magnifying glass, you can sometimes see dust, just floating in the air."

"Why doesn't the dust kill us?" Brian asked.

"The dust isn't harmful. If it were, there would be no people on Earth. But the virus is harmful—and contagious, and that makes it dangerous. That's why we have to find out how to fight it. How to keep the virus from attacking the cells inside our bodies."

"What if you could see the virus?" Brian wondered. "If you could see it, you could run away from it."

"Then it wouldn't be a virus," his mom said. "It would be something else."

Because they were stuck inside their house, Brian's parents did what they could to keep his spirits up and his nightmares down. He was sad that he couldn't have a birthday party when he turned five, but he was excited to learn he could get any present he wanted. That's what his parents promised.

Brian spent a lot of time thinking about it. Did he want a new bike? A scooter? A big box of Legos? Magnets that could be made into a house or car? Maybe they'd let him see movies that they had told him he wasn't old enough to see yet, like *The Wizard of Oz, Snow White and the Seven Dwarfs, Pinocchio, Spiderman,* Batman, or any of the Transporter or Avenger or X-Men movies he had heard about from his older cousins. His parents *did* say *anything.*

After a few days of thought, Brian told his parents what he wanted for his birthday.

"A magnifying glass."

"Interesting," his dad said. "Why that?"

"Then I can set a trap for the virus and look at it with the magnifying glass. Then I'll know what it looks like, so I can run away from it if it comes after me."

"As long as we stay in the house and don't go out without wearing a mask and keep away from other people, the virus won't go after you. But it's a good idea to want to know as much as you can about it."

"How come you go out, Dad? You should stay home with us."

"I only go out when I have to, because that's my job. They let me work at home most of the time, but once a week they want me to go in and take care of things that I can't do here."

On the day the magnifying glass arrived in the mail, the virus had infected over eight million people worldwide, and killed over 200,000 in the U.S. alone. Brian didn't pay any attention to such numbers; his focus was on cutting two-inch squares of cardboard and taping them into boxes that he called virus traps. He poked tiny needle holes on the top of each box to catch the virus. When he showed them to his parents, they were impressed with his diligence and his determination.

"Only one problem," his dad said. "If the virus gets in through those holes, what stops it from getting out the same way?"

"Because," Brian said, "there are so many viruses that once they get in, they'll be pushed down by others coming in and that's how they'll be trapped."

"And how will you see them without them getting on you?" his mom asked.

"I'll wear my mask and look through my magnifying glass."

"Sounds like a plan," Dad said.

Brian stapled pieces of string on several boxes and hung one from the lampshade in their living room, and another from a low tree limb in the backyard. He also placed one in the corner of his closet next to his sneakers and asked his mom to put one on top of the refrigerator in the kitchen. With them all in place, he went outside to look at insects and fallen leaves with his magnifying glass.

His parents were relieved that Brian had found things to do on his own. He was still too young to sit still at the computer for Zoom time with classmates and friends, and it wasn't easy to keep him entertained throughout the day. If the virus taught them anything, it was an appreciation for his pre-school teachers.

Every day, the boy checked his traps, looking intensely at the small holes with his magnifying glass. He couldn't see into the boxes, so there was no real way he could tell if he had caught a virus. But after four days of checking in the morning, after lunch, and before dinner, he heard a small sound in the box that hung from the tree. He quickly took it down, placed the trap in a plastic container, and told his parents that he had done it. He had captured the virus.

"Did you see it?" his mom asked.

"It's there," Brian said. "I heard it."

"Have you looked inside?"

"Isn't that dangerous?"

"You're right, it could be."

When his dad came home from his one-day-a-week trip to his office, Brian showed him the container. "Look what I got," Brian said with the pride of a child who had done something good.

"Let me see," his dad said, lifting the top of Brian's trap.

"Close it! Close it! It's the virus. You're letting it out!"

His father put the lid back on and rubbed Brian's head. "Congratulations," he said. "One of these days you're going to grow up and become a great scientist. You'll find how to cure diseases."

"That's what I'll do on my sixth birthday," Brian said. "Or maybe when I'm really old, like ten or something."

"One day, you can save the world!" his dad said. "And we can say it started when you got the magnifying glass you asked for on your fifth birthday."

That night, Brian's head was full of what he was going to do when he got bigger. Finding the virus was just the beginning. Next, he had to figure out how to make it go away, so people could go outside again, kids could go to school and play in the park, and grownups could go to the movies and shop for toys for their children. He was proud of himself and told his parents that they didn't have to worry about the virus because he would figure out a way to make it disappear.

His happiness lasted for a few days, but then his father started coughing. His temperature began to rise, he got chills, and when he couldn't taste the fruit his wife cut, he suspected he had COVID-19. His wife asked their neighbor to keep an eye on their house and left Brian inside so she could drive her husband to a nearby testing location.

The test was positive. "Dad has the virus," Brian's mom said to him.

"Did I give it to him?" Brian asked. "When he opened the container?"

"No, darling, you didn't. He must have gotten it when he went out. A lot of people have it, that's why it's so important for us not to go out."

"Will Daddy get better?"

"I hope so. We'll pray for him."

But God wasn't listening to all the prayers directed His way. Soon, Dad had trouble breathing and had to be hospitalized. He was put on a ventilator for three days. And then he died.

Brian didn't understand death. He just knew that his dad wasn't coming back from the hospital. He and his mom were allowed to go to the funeral home where his dad was cremated, but Brian was too young to be told about that. After they said their goodbyes, his mom took him for ice cream. And when they returned home, Brian went to the backyard, found a rock and broke the magnifying glass.

"I don't want to see it, I never want to see it," he cried. "I want it to be invisible. I want my Daddy back. I didn't mean it. I didn't."

"It's not your fault," his mother said. "You didn't catch the virus in those traps. It was a bug that got inside, that's what you heard."

"No, it wasn't a bug. It was the *virus*. I *know* it was."

Brian's grief broke his mother's heart. She had to be strong for him. But she wasn't strong enough. A week after the funeral, she got the cough. Then the fever. Her progression mirrored her husband's. Next, the chills, the headaches, and the inability to tell a mango from a banana. When it was her turn to be hospitalized, her sister, Brian's aunt, came to stay with Brian. And when his mother died, Brian was told that she would have to be in the hospital for a long time.

"Why don't you come live with me until she's better?" his aunt suggested. "We'll bring your clothes and your toys, and you'll have your cousins to play with."

But Brian knew his mother wasn't ever coming home. He knew she had gone to be with his daddy. He knew that he had given them both the virus.

"Brian, honey, what do you think? Would you like to do that?"

"Where do they go?" he asked.

"What did your mom say?"

"That we go to heaven when we die."

"That's right."

"So, Mommy went to be with Daddy?"

"Oh, Brian. We're all going to be together again one day."

"What if you do something bad, do you still go to heaven?"

"God is very forgiving. But your parents never did anything bad."

Brian didn't want to talk about what he was thinking. After his aunt kissed him goodnight, he got out of bed and went to his closet, where he had hidden his virus traps in a paper bag. He took the one that his dad had opened and put it to his face. He lifted the top, inhaled, and licked the inside of the small box.

Then he returned to his bed, closed his eyes, and hoped that he could find his mother and father in heaven.

HOLD ME

"Look at it this way, you'll get a chance to Make-A-Wish," Sophia's dad, Carter, said.

"Not funny," Sophia said.

"Anything you want: A wish away. And you're *going* to recover."

"I don't know what I want, except get better," Sophia said, and shrugged, her small shoulders rising up by her ears.

"You will get better, honey. I promise. You have the strength. The determination. The will. And so do I. And so did your mom. I love you; I will always be there for you, you know how…."

"I want to hug an octopus," Sophia said.

"…I feel…… You what?" her dad asked, caught in mid-sentence by her strange request.

"That's my wish."

"You have the chance to meet any pop star in the world or get a trip to any theme park of your choice or ride an elephant. It's a great organization; they will go out of their way to grant your wish."

"So, you think they'll find me an octopus to hug, and to be hugged back?"

"No idea, Soph. Can only ask."

"Wouldn't that be something if I could? You know how smart they are?"

"Compared to a whale? A crow? A chimp?"

"Smarter. I've read two books about them. They're *really* smart, Dad. They know things."

Sophia's fascination with cephalopods began after she had been diagnosed and found, at the hospital library, a book about these mysterious sea creatures. She then found videos about them on the Internet. When she saw how deftly an octopus could escape from its tank in a lab, shimmy through a heating duct to another room where some of its favorite fish swam in a tank, grab a snack, and shimmy back to its own tank, she was hooked. She couldn't get enough of watching these Houdinis of the sea. How they could transform, disguising themselves in plain sight, changing colors and shapes, making their skin smooth or lumpy, multitasking with their tentacles. They were not just great escape artists, but magicians, strategists, with remarkable survival instincts. If she could return in another life, she hoped it could be as an octopus. Though they didn't live long, they certainly lived exciting, adventurous, and playful lives; the kind of living she would have liked to experience if she hadn't been cursed with a fatal disease. She was fifteen years old and had never been kissed; never skied or snowboarded; never played soccer or run a marathon; never took a hallucinogenic drug. Just imagine what she could have done with eight arms, three hearts, and nine brains.

That's what she thought about while the drug cocktail dripped slowly into her body. What would it be like to *be* an octopus? Not one of the small ones, but the Great Pacific one. A cephalopod that reached the size of a giraffe, looking as alien as anything on the planet, yet so functional that in three hundred million years it barely genetically mutated.

A Great Pacific octopus would be too large to embrace, but now that she had settled on a wish, she began to look for what size octopus might be right for her. There were hundreds of species, ranging from the golf ball sized Blue Ring octopus, whose venom could kill two dozen people within minutes, to the rarely seen Seven Arm octopus, a cousin of the Great Pacific, but much less understood. Among the eight large species, five were too big for her. The other three grew to be between three and four-and-a-half feet, certainly within huggable range. There was the Southern Red, the Yellow, and the Common. Those were where to start, she told her dad. If he could get in touch with a local aquarium, maybe he could find out if such a wish were even possible.

"Do you have any idea how strong an octopus's grip can be?" the chief biologist of the city's aquarium asked Carter. "For any of the large size cephalopods, each of their suction cup suckers can lift over thirty pounds. And since they have hundreds of suckers on each of their tentacles, try to imagine what it might be like if one decided to use such strength in an embrace."

"Guess that puts a kibosh on my daughter's wish," Carter said.

"Is she terminal?" the biologist asked.

"Yes, but I don't tell her that. She's got a great spirit."

"What does her mother think?"

"We lost her to the virus a while ago. It's just the two of us."

"Sorry to hear. Maybe you can bring her here after closing time and she can meet one of the smaller ones. She can put her hand in the tank, feel what it's like to have a tentacle wrap around her wrist."

Sophia was game to be able to touch an octopus, but it wasn't what she wanted as her one wish. The wish had to be special; it had to be something no one else had ever experienced.

"It's gonna be tough," her dad said. "These are unpredictable creatures. The staff at the aquarium has to be very cautious around them."

"Maybe we shouldn't be looking at aquariums," Sophia said. "Maybe we could find marine biologists who are studying octopuses in their laboratories."

Carter looked at his daughter with love, pride, and deep sadness. She was the light in his darkness. He would do anything for her. But could he pull off finding someone who happened to have a large octopus floating in a tank that could be lifted out of the water so that his daughter could hold it?

The Make-A-Wish people said it was the most unusual wish any child had ever made, but they didn't say it was impossible. They had no idea what could or could not be done when it came to hugging an octopus. They had a large network and began making inquiries.

It wasn't the kind of wish that could be fulfilled easily or quickly. Sometimes, when a child asked to meet a favorite athlete or film star, it could take weeks or longer to coordinate a time that fit both their schedules. But if the child began failing, the meeting could be more simply arranged online, lifting the child's spirit in a personal, one-on-one moment.

But Sophia's wish could not come through Skype or Zoom. And it veered toward being dangerous, which made it all the more challenging.

In the end, it was Sophia who found a biologist named Warren Hull, who studied the smaller of the large cephalopods. When her father explained her circumstances and that all expenses to make her wish happen would be covered by the Make-A-Wish Foundation, Hull invited them to visit his lab, which was only thirty miles from the hospital. "I can't make any promises," he warned, "because these animals are extremely sensitive, they are capable of experiencing joy, anger, fear, love, and their suction cups have chemoreceptors, so they can taste what they touch. I've seen them cuddle up to one person and hide from another."

"Understood," Carter said. "I'm not that crazy about her doing this, so if the octopus doesn't like the way she tastes, that's fine. At least we'll have tried."

"It won't happen on the first visit," Hull said. "An octopus has to warm up to you. The first time, if all goes well, she'll let your daughter touch her. Maybe she'll touch back. If she does, then you can come back and see how the octopus responds. It could take five or ten visits before any kind of holding might happen."

Make-A-Wish arranged for a van to take Sophia and Carter to Hull's lab. They worked with the hospital staff to provide a bed and the chemical drip for Sophia while she was there. Sophia went with no trepidation, just pure excitement. She asked a nurse to scrub her extra clean, hoping that the octopus would not taste or smell the poisons dripping into her body. She weighed under a hundred pounds and looked younger than her age, but the sparkle in her eyes and the smile on her face made all who helped get her to the lab feel they were doing something special.

There were three tanks in the lab, each housing a different species—the Yellow was the largest at four-and-a-half feet, weighing eleven pounds; the Southern Red was three feet, eight pounds; the Common was two-and-a-half feet, twelve pounds. Of the three, the one that took to Sophia was the Southern Red.

"We call her Ginger," Hull said. "She's the sweetest of the three. I'm a bit surprised that she came right to you."

"Can I touch her?" Sophia asked.

"First, let's feed her a fish." He took a small fish from a bucket and gave it to Sophia. "Put it near one of her tentacles. If she takes it, she'll slide it up her suckers like an escalator until it reaches her beak. Then she'll swallow it."

Sophia leaned towards the tank from her bed and slowly brought the fish to Ginger, who didn't hesitate. "She must be hungry," Sophia said.

After Ginger devoured the fish, Sophia was allowed to put her hand in the tank water. Ginger touched her fingers with two tentacles. Sophia felt a new sensation. Not just in her hand, but throughout her body. It was almost as if Ginger was trying to communicate with her.

"Probably enough for today," Warren Hull said. But when Sophia began to remove her hand, Ginger pulled on it, holding her for a moment. Sophia smiled happily.

"I think she likes me."

"This went well," Hull said.

"Can we come back tomorrow?" Sophia asked.

"If it's all right with your doctors, I don't see why not."

Her doctors had no objections, because there was nothing more they could do for her. It was their consensus that the chemo wasn't working, and that she should be taken off the regimen and allowed to die at her own pace. When the pain set in, there would be morphine.

Over the following weeks, Sophia and Ginger bonded, hand to tentacles. But it was more than that. Sophia sensed that Ginger knew what was going on with her, that she was dying. But though Sophia worried about her father and how he would handle her death so soon after her mother's passing, she also couldn't suppress the elation she felt when she was with Ginger. It was as if she had made a new best friend, a friend that understood her—what she was thinking, what she was feeling.

An octopus was a highly complex creature, one had even learned how to use a camera to take pictures of his keeper, but Ginger seemed to possess telepathic powers. She couldn't speak, but when she wrapped a tentacle around Sophia's arm, it was as if they became one, sharing each other's thoughts. Ginger somehow made Sophia realize that it was going to be all right for her to let go, that she would soon be free of her painful, fragile body. Ginger helped Sophia remain calm during this time.

With each visit, Warren Hull could see how Sophia was getting weaker. He could see the toll these visits took on her father Carter, who bravely strove to keep a positive attitude. "I think Ginger might be ready for that hug," he said on a day when father and daughter looked like they needed a lift.

"Really?" Sophia said, rubbing her mother's small pendant of St. Francis that she wore on a string around her neck. It didn't protect her mother, and she didn't believe it would protect her, but she wore it to keep her mother close. "I think so too. I think we're both ready."

Hull carefully put both hands into the tank and grabbed Ginger under her tentacles. Her large head swayed side to side until Hull was able to balance her. Sophia stood next to him and when she opened her arms, Ginger spread her eight tentacles to embrace her friend. Hull kept Ginger's head from flopping until Sophia managed to take the octopus against her chest by herself. Her father couldn't hold back his tears as he watched, and videoed, this incredible moment. Ginger's tentacles surrounded Sophia, her large eyes looking into Sophia's eyes. Sophia spoke softly to Ginger, as the octopus tightened her grip. "I'm ready," she whispered. "I'm not afraid."

Warren Hull saw Ginger's color change from red to white, the color of Sophia's blouse, and saw how Sophia's body was being crushed by their embrace. He moved to grab one of Ginger's tentacles, but he couldn't budge it.

"What's happening?" Carter shouted.

"She won't let go," Hull said, trying to pull Ginger by her head.

"Stop," Sophia whispered, holding on to Ginger. "Leave her alone."

And then, finally, the octopus released her, and Sophia slumped to the floor.

Warren Hull was distraught. He knew what had happened, and it was his fault. He never should have let Ginger embrace Sophia. Something like that should have taken at least six months to a year to prepare for. Carter leaned down to take his daughter in his arms. He rocked her back and forth. "It's okay," he cried. "You're free. You're with your mother. You'll take care of each other."

After the funeral, Carter returned to Hull's lab and they watched the video Carter had recorded on his phone. They could see, in slow motion, the look in both Sophia and Ginger's eyes, as if they were communicating intuitively. They watched as Sophia whispered into Ginger's ear, and then Ginger began to tighten her grip as her color changed and the two became one. There was Sophia's smile of relief; and Ginger's soulful stare.

"What do you want to do with her?" Hull asked.

"What do you mean?" Carter said.

"Should I put her down?"

"No, of course not," Carter said. And then he asked if he could touch her.

"Are you sure? After what she did?"

"She knew what she was doing," Carter said. "They both did."

Carter put his hand into the tank, and Ginger swam to him and wrapped a tentacle around his wrist.

"Thank you," Carter said.

The octopus looked up at him, uncurled a different tentacle, and placed the St. Francis pendant in his hand.

A MARRIAGE

"Did you take your pills?"

"I forgot."

"You always forget. Why can't you put your pills out the day before, like I do, so they're there and you won't forget?"

"Why do you always tell me what to do?"

"I'm just saying…"

"You say too much. Take your pills. Wash the dishes in the sink, not the dishwasher. Wear sandals to walk. Don't do so much laundry, it will ruin the machine. Do you ever listen to yourself?"

"If you would ever listen to me, I wouldn't have to keep repeating myself."

"How many years has it been that you've been telling me what to do, what to read, what to watch, when to walk, how to exercise? Fifty?"

"You want me to stop? Try listening once in a while. See if I'm right."

"You're always right. You're never wrong. If I die, who will you have to nag? To blame?"

"I don't nag. I just say something when I see something to talk to you about. You, on the other hand, don't ever say anything."

"Maybe because you talk enough for the two of us. You ever hear yourself talk? We visit our friends, you do all the talking. Maybe that's why we don't have so many friends anymore."

"What are you talking about? We don't go out because your silence makes people uncomfortable. They ask you something, you answer with two words, not even a sentence."

"I wish you could learn how to communicate with fewer words. You talk in paragraphs. And you tell the same stories."

"Not to the same people."

"Yes, to the same people. They listen because they don't remember anything you tell them. You're just background noise."

"That's ridiculous."

"You think so? I don't think so. I think you should try not talking so much and see how that goes."

"Why don't you go read a book."

"See, there you go. Telling me what to do."

"Okay, so let's go for a walk."

"I don't want to."

"You never want to."

"I'll walk on the treadmill. It's too hot outside."

"So, we should walk in the morning."

"I do my exercise in the morning."

"Before you exercise."

"Stop already! You don't let up."

A scene from Elana and Yousef's marriage. Which one is Elana, which Yousef? Does it matter? This is how they communicate. Fifty years together, they still go at it over one percent vs. two-percent milk. Fat vs. non-fat yogurt. Baked vs. fried chicken. Anti-perspirant vs. aluminum free deodor-ant. Organic vs. non-organic fruits and vegetables. On-line vs. store shopping.

Elana's the quiet one. She takes care of the house, she does the cooking, she likes to garden, go to the farmer's mar-ket, have a coffee by herself. Yousef watches over her, wants to make sure she's aware of sales and discounts, loves her in his own way.

And then came the pandemic. The mayor and the gov-ernor said stay at home, don't go out, wash your hands, wear a mask, and keep your distance from others. The times they were away from each other, even if it was just a few hours out, is what made their marriage work. They didn't know this until they couldn't get away from each other. Until they were stuck in their house, twenty-four hours a day, seven days a week, for months. And yet, even though they listened to the mayor and governor, Elana still got the virus.

"How is it possible? Did you get it at the farmer's market? I told you not to go. We don't always have to have fresh veg-etables. Or did you open a package and forget to wash your hands? You always forget to wash your hands. And you never wash your face. Water is not enough. You splash yourself and think you're clean."

"You going to blame me now? When I'm sick? When I may die? Am I going to have to hear you complaining all day?"

"I'm sorry, El, really. It's shitty that you got it. It's shitty that you have to stay in the guest room with the door shut. I'll take care of everything."

"You don't know how to cook; how are you going to take care of me?"

"I'll make things. I'll order in. We'll manage."

To the surprises of both of them, they managed better than they thought they would. With the door closed, Elana found that she could read the books she wanted to without Yousef's constant interruptions, like when he would come to read her something about vitamins or how to properly wash vegetables, or shout for her to look at something he found cute or funny on the Internet. The peace she found in quarantine was worth the fever and the head and body aches. As for her loss of taste, it didn't matter, considering the bland or over-spiced food Yousef cooked.

Each morning, when Yousef put her toast and jam and cup of coffee by her door, he would ask, "You okay today? You get enough sleep? Do you need to go to the hospital yet?"

He was annoying, but, in his own way, loving. As much as he nagged, his heart was in the right place. He didn't want to lose her. He would be lost without her. And though she often thought that it would be nice to take separate vacations, she knew Yousef would be miserable without her, and maybe she would feel the same way. Theirs was a marriage like any other marriage, with ups and downs, petty annoyances and disagreements, but never outright quarrels. They had learned to live with each other, to tolerate the other as best they could. Elana knew that, because he was an atheist, Yousef didn't pray, but she was sure he was praying for her now.

The virus didn't kill Elana. It was an unpleasant but peaceful two-week break from her husband, who missed her cooking, her forgetfulness, and her body next to his at night.

After she recovered, she spent another two weeks in isolation, to make sure the virus didn't return. If it did, and she gave it to Yousef, it would kill him, for sure. She was convinced of that. He didn't have her strength.

"Good to see you again," Yousef said a month later, when she came out from behind the closed door.

"And you, too," Elana said. "I knew if I could survive your lousy coffee, I could beat the virus."

"What was wrong with my coffee? I used a filter, just like you do."

"You didn't use enough coffee. And you didn't warm the milk."

"So why didn't you say anything?"

"I was weak, Yousef. I wasn't myself."

"You're never yourself. If you don't complain, how am I to know? It's typical, you won't change. You don't listen, you don't complain. What am I going to do with you?"

"Better this way," Elana said. "What would you do without me?"

TURN THE SPIT ON THAT PIG

I couldn't wait for the weekend. Marta was cooking up a surprise dinner; four of her closest friends, and me. I looked forward to it all week. Bought a Silver Oak Cabernet Sauvignon wine, two six-packs of Guinness beer, and a strawberry cheesecake from my favorite Sweet Mary Jane bakery. Wanted to make a good impression.

Marta was the girl I'd been hoping to find. There'd been a few I thought might work out, but it's hard to meet someone you might get along with in sickness and health for the rest of your life. Practically impossible, when you think about it.

In my high school yearbook, a half dozen friends commented that they expected me and Marianne would make it to the altar, but that ended when she got into Notre Dame and I went to Brandeis. In college, I fell for Darlene, and all my mother could say about her was that I found the only *shiksa* in a predominantly Jewish school. We laughed about that, but after two years going together, it turned out my mother was right. Darlene wouldn't remove the cross from her neck when we made love, and I couldn't adjust to being with someone who believed that cross was more than just a piece of jewelry.

During my junior year abroad, when I studied at Keio University in Tokyo, I met another foreign student, Carmen, from Brazil. We clicked from the get-go, but that may have had more to do with the fact that we were both thousands of miles from our homes and welcomed the comfort of being strangers in a strange land together. But I didn't go to Japan to study Portuguese, and she wasn't there to learn English. Our common language was sex, and whatever rudimentary Japanese we were able to pick up.

And now, there's Marta. Another non-Jew, that's true. But other than that, she checks off all the other boxes. She's lively, independent, a gourmet cook, with advanced degrees in Art History and Economics. She's read all the writers I've read, likes the same blues singers, rock bands, and jazz groups as I do, and shares similar feelings about movies as diverse as Bergman's *Persona* and *The Lord of the Rings* trilogy.

As for her friends, I met them when Saturday came around.

When she introduced me to Elliott, she said he was her best friend. He was one of her roommates in college, and she warned me that I had to pass his approval. "He's tough on the guys I date," Marta said. "But he's going to love you."

Alicia was her other roommate, and Marta told me that Alicia didn't trust men in general, and though she would smile sweetly and make interesting small talk, I should be careful what I said about women in general around her.

Her other two besties were Frank and his girlfriend, Sandy. They were both in the residency phase of their medical careers. Frank was on track to becoming a dermatologist and Sandy an Ob/Gyn. I had never met young doctors before and was a bit nervous trying to think of things to say to them.

"Silver Oak," Elliott said when I put down the wine. "I love this wine, good choice."

"Hope you like Guinness, too," I said. "Some people think it's too dark."

"Not much of a beer drinker," he said. "I'll stick to the wine."

"I like Guinness," Sandy said. "It's one of the healthier beers. The Irish drink it like water."

"Have you been to Ireland?" I asked.

"No," she said. "Have you?"

"I've never made it to Europe," I said.

"David spent a year in Japan," Marta shouted from the far side of her garden. She was preparing a twenty-pound pig to roast on a turnspit.

"You need some help with that?" Elliott asked.

"In a few minutes," she said. "David, why don't you tell them some of the stories you told me about Tokyo?"

"You mean the ones about the drunks peeing in the street and in the subway?" I asked.

"I'd rather not hear that," Alicia said.

"Can't say I blame you," I said. I was already on edge meeting these people, and seeing Marta stuffing tomatoes, onions, garlic cloves and all sorts of fresh herbs and dried spices into the pig's chest cavity made me queasy. Truth be told, I had never eaten pork. Not even a BLT. It was considered *tref* in our home, something the goyim ate, but not us Conservative Jews. I rejected the idea of a Supreme Being long ago, and I didn't consider myself religious in any way, but for reasons I couldn't explain, let alone articulate, the thought of eating a pig made me nauseous. And yet, there was Marta, making this special dinner in my honor, showing me off to her hip best friends.

"What's your favorite part of the pig?" Sandy asked Marta.

"Who doesn't like loin?" Marta answered. "But I'm also fond of the cheek."

"I'm a shoulder man," Elliott said. "How about you, David?"

Wish he hadn't asked me that. There was no part of a pig that was my favorite. But I didn't want to put a damper on this party, so I said, "I'm with Marta."

Once Marta finished stuffing the animal, which she said she got from an organic farm, she asked for some help while she sewed up the cavity with baling wire.

"This is impressive," I said, looking at the steel pipe she had fitted through the pig's anus and out the mouth. There was a dirt pit filled with burning charcoals and wood, and cinder blocks which would be used to balance the handle on the pipe once it was lifted three feet above the pit. "A lot of work to roast old Porky."

"Sure is," Marta said. "But worth it. Wait till you taste it."

"Can't wait," I lied. And then, my nerves got the best of me and I started making whatever pig jokes I could remember, like "Why do they call it a pig pen? Why not a pencil?" and, "Do you know who the smartest pig was? Ein-swine."

When neither of those got a laugh, I tried some others.

"What do you get when you cross a pig with a dinosaur? Jurassic Pork."

Nothing.

"What's pig's favorite play? *Hamlet*."

More nothing. These people were obviously not into making fun of the food they were about to eat.

"A pig with laryngitis? Disgruntled. A pig thief? A hamburglar."

I couldn't stop. The greater their silence, the harder I tried. And then, I topped myself with this: "A woman enters a bar with a parrot on her shoulder. The bartender says, 'You can't bring that pig in here.' The woman says, 'It's not a pig, you idiot, it's a parrot.' And the bartender says, 'I was talking to the parrot.'"

Thud.

Oh boy, a woman-as-pig joke in the age of #MeToo. Alice looked at me as if I had just personally insulted her. Marta tried to save me. "I've got one," she said. "What's the difference between Donald Trump and a flying pig?"

This time, her friends looked interested. And when she responded, "The letter F," everyone laughed. That was a good pig joke. And that's why I felt she was the right woman for me. Added to her other qualities, she was able to step in and save me from drowning.

It took two-and-a-half hours to roast the pig, with each of us having a go at turning the spit every fifteen minutes. As the pig cooked, Marta sang the pig lyric from that Tom Waits song as she basted it with a garlic and lemon sauce, and in the end gave it a once-over with a walnut honey glaze. There was no apple in the pig's mouth, but, aesthetically, I wish there had been. In fact, I wish the damn thing had caught fire and we didn't have to eat it.

"Ever treated anyone with trichinosis?" I asked Frank and Sandy.

"Never," Sandy said. "It's pretty rare. Happens more often with bear meat."

"Outside of Alaska, who eats bear?" I wondered.

"You'd be surprised," Frank said. "People eat all sorts of meat."

"What's your favorite?" I asked him.

"What we're having looks pretty good to me," he said.

"Amen to that," said Alicia. "I'm starving."

It took another hour or so for Marta to carve up the pig and we all grabbed plates. I let them take whatever choice parts they preferred, hoping I might get away with some bread, salad and corn before dessert. But Marta saved what she called a buttery slice of loin just for me. I thanked her, looked at how it covered most of the plate, and sat down at the end of the table. I thought if I fiddled with it for a while, I might give the impression that I was eating it.

"Hmmm, so good," Sandy said.

"This is the best I've ever eaten," Elliott said. "You've outdone yourself."

Alicia and Frank piped in as well, complimenting the chef on how tender the meat was, how perfect the glaze, and how crispy the skin.

"You like it?" Marta asked me.

I hadn't tried it yet, but she was looking at me, smiling, and I nodded my head as I cut into the loin. I put the meat in my mouth and gave a thumbs up as I chewed. Then I took a gulp of Guinness to get it down. And that's how I ate my first pork meal. A small bite, a large swallow of beer; another small bite, another large gulp. I managed to clean my plate and drink two bottles of beer and a glass of wine. I wish I could say I liked it, but I was too disgusted with myself to give the pig a chance. For me, this was an act of love. Eating Marta's *tref* was something I would not have done for any other woman in my past.

As the others talked and shared stories, I sat quietly, wishing the night would end so I could go home and try to throw up. What was wrong with me? Why was eating this meal such a big deal? I knew it was psychological, and I knew that I had somehow violated a principle that I had carried throughout my life. Maybe it was a good thing. Maybe I was broadening my horizons. Maybe I was ready to make a commitment to life, to experience, to adventure. Maybe I was even ready to settle down and have this amazing woman be my wife and the mother of our children.

The cheesecake helped get rid of the taste of pig in my mouth, and I was proud of myself that I didn't rush into the house to upchuck in Marta's bathroom. But I think her friends could tell that I wasn't a happy camper.

"Are you Jewish?" Alicia asked.

"Guilty," I tried to joke.

"Not really much of a pork eater, are you?"

"How could you tell?"

"You stopped with the jokes once the meal was served."

"Ah, well."

"Hey, man," Elliott said, "the wine was great. Nice touch."

"I should have brought another bottle," I said.

"We all got a taste. And the beer seemed to help you get through this."

"You noticed?"

"Hey, good for you, know what I'm saying?"

"Thanks. Appreciated."

When the party broke up, Marta wanted me to spend the night. But I thought enough was enough, I needed to be on my own. We kissed goodnight, our breaths smelling of the meat we had eaten, and she said, "See you tomorrow?"

"I don't know," I answered. "Maybe."

What the hell was that? The woman had spent an entire day preparing for this evening and I brushed her off with a "Maybe" as if I had just met her.

She looked at me and I could see that the sparkle in her eyes had faded.

"That joke about Trump," I said. "That was funny."

"It wasn't mine," she said. "I heard it somewhere."

"Still," I said.

And that was it. The last thing I ever said to Marta. But I did turn the spit on that pig.

WHERE THE HYENAS ROAM

For three hours every afternoon, the Hyena Man collected bones from a dozen restaurants in Addis Ababa, so he'd have enough for his evening show. The restaurant owners participated because the hyenas attracted tourists, and tourists ate at restaurants. There was usually enough meat left on the bones to let the hyenas smell when it was feeding time. The Hyena Man didn't charge anything, but the tourists who came to the outskirts of the city to witness this ritual never failed to put money in his bucket.

The hyenas knew him as Bone Feeder and came to understand that if they left him alone, he'd return the next evening with more bones. There were other hyena men in Ethiopia, but most did it for the money. Some put on more of a show, sticking a piece of meat on the end of a stick, with the other end in their mouths, or letting a hyena sit on top of them as they lay on their backs with meat between their teeth. But the Hyena Man cared more for the animals than the tips.

The hyenas, though, didn't really care who came to offer them food. They just liked to eat, whether it was the rotting carcass of a gazelle or wildebeest, the fresh kill of a bush pig or dik-dik, or whatever garbage or dung they could scavenge. They were strong, nasty tempered animals whose powerful jaws could crush any sized bone. Their leader went by the name Sharpy.

"I smell kudu," Sharpy snarled, and the pack lifted their noses. Fresh killed kudu was in the air.

They followed Sharpy's lead as he ran in that hobbled way his kind ran.

"Wild dogs," one of the hyenas said. "That's what took it down."

"Dogs will not replace us!" Sharpy bellowed, and his pack repeated his cry. "But I think it's wolves."

"Wolves will not replace us!" the pack shouted.

"Branch out, surround that kill," Sharpy instructed. "Dogs or wolves, we'll chase them away."

But when they approached the site where the kudu lay, they saw that it had been a cheetah that took it down and was trying to get her mouth around its neck so she could drag it up a tree. The hyenas became emboldened by their numbers and the cheetah had a decision to make.

"Cheetahs will not replace us!" the hyenas howled.

The cheetah dropped the kudu, growled at the animal snatchers, and ran off.

The hyenas moved in and ripped the kudu apart, feasting on the meat and bones.

Outside of Addis Ababa, the Hyena Man sat with his basket of bones, making clucking sounds to call the pack, but they were too far off to hear him. And besides, they were stuffing themselves on fresh kill.

The fifteen tourists, with their cameras and cell phones, were getting restless as dusk turned to darkness. They had come in three separate minivans and had each paid the drivers 750 birr, the equivalent of twenty dollars each, to bring them to see this old man in a worn leather jacket and weathered cloth pants, with a white skullcap on his head, demonstrate his fearlessness with wild spotted hyenas. The three drivers knew that if the animals didn't show up, they'd have to refund the money but that rarely happened. Hyenas were among the great scavengers in the animal kingdom, and even when they had eaten their fill, they'd still go to where the offering took no effort on their part.

"How much longer must we wait?" an English woman asked. "It's getting chilly."

"These things can't be timed exactly," one of the drivers said. "But they will come. They always come."

And, eventually, they came. The first thing the tourists saw was the shining eyes. They seemed to glow in the dark from fifty yards out. Then there was the shuffling of their gait. And then, the sharp teeth, the harsh faces, the hunched shoulders. These were not pretty animals. They looked mean, surly, unfriendly. They had chased away a cheetah and were prepared to take on wild dogs or a wolf pack, and now they were coming to snack on some bones and have their pictures taken.

But the Hyena Man sensed something was different about them on this evening. Besides being an hour late, their mouths dripped blood, and their leader had a look in his eyes that caused the Hyena Man to shout out in Amharic that the people should move away, towards the vans. But only the drivers understood what he was shouting, and they didn't want to spoil the show.

"Get back, get back!" the Hyena Man shouted.

"What's he saying?" a French tourist asked.

"That's just his crazy talk, how he deals with the hyenas," one of the drivers said. "Nothing to worry about."

When the hyenas surrounded Bone Feeder, they waited to see what Sparky would do. Was this the day he would call them to attack the hand that fed them? Maybe the time had come to go after all those who stood on two legs, with their stupid-looking faces and chemical body smells. Would their battle cry be "Two-Legs will not replace us!"?

Bone Feeder clacked two large bones together and spoke to them in Amharic. Sparky's back legs dragged behind his large, muscled body as he stuck his bloody face inches from Bone Feeder. The old man didn't flinch. He had no name for this hyena, but he had developed a relationship of trust with him over the years. They seemed to have a good sense of each other, and the Hyena Man believed that he understood this animal as well as any human could understand a 120-pound hyena. The old Ethiopian put the bones to Sparky's nose and waited. Cameras clicked to capture the tense moment. And when Sparky opened his jaw to take both bones, his fellow hyenas seemed to relax. They approached Bone Feeder, who knew that had their leader refused the bones they might have tried to attack him, and each of them got something from his basket.

"Is it always so fraughtful?" an American teenager asked.

"Yes, yes, always like this," a driver answered.

"This is my third time," a Swiss tourist said, "and I've never seen such tension before. This was scary."

"Well," the teenager said, "they *are* wild hyenas."

Sparky seemed to comprehend that these Two-Legged's were talking about him and his brethren and wondered how they'd react to some snarling, growling, and bared teeth. So, he gave it a shot and watched as the Two Legs' jumped back in fear. He could smell their anxiety.

And then he got shot. The drivers all carried guns, just in case there was an incident like this, and one of them pulled his and fired. Sparky yelped and the other hyenas scattered, running off to regroup.

"Get in the vans!" the drivers all commanded, and the tourists piled in. But not the Hyena Man. He stood up and went to Sparky, to see how badly he had been wounded.

"We trusted you," Sparky's eyes said.

"You scared them," the old man said.

"They will not replace us," Sparky's eyes said.

"No, no one will replace you," the old man said. "You have been here before us and you will be here after we're gone."

"We will take what is yours," Sparky's eyes said. "We will take what is the dogs, the wolves, the cheetahs, and the lions. Nothing will replace us."

"Tell that to the Jew," the old man said. But Sparky stopped listening to the Bone Feeder. The bullet had entered his shoulder, just behind his head, and he felt weak.

"You'll survive," the Hyena Man said, mixing some herbs from his bag with a handful of dirt to plug the hole in the hyena's shoulder. "You'll be back. And I'll have bones for you."

"We're not going anywhere," Sparky's eyes said. "This is our land."

TOMORROW

"**W**hat are you going to do with your dad today?" Grandpa Bill asked his grandson after they finished their Zoom reading of *The Wizard of Oz*, a book the boy's mother said kept him up at night.

"I'll tell you tomorrow," he answered.

Such a smart kid. He had no idea what his father had in mind for the afternoon. He could just as easily have said, "We're going to play." Or, "Drawing." Or, "Read another book." Or, "Maybe we'll watch TV." He knew his dad would feed him, so he could have speculated what food they might eat. But he was a wise child and preferred to keep their options open.

Later, when his father suggested they take a walk around the neighborhood, the boy got his scooter, put on his helmet, and reminded his dad to bring a water bottle.

"So, what did you think of the book Grandpa read you?"

"I didn't know why the China people got broken."

"Are there Chinese people in *The Wizard of Oz*?"

"They were smaller than me, but there was a wall, and the Scarecrow and the Tin Man and Dorothy had to stand on the Lion to get over, and then they landed on the China people and broke them. Then the flying monkeys had to come and take them away from the scary people with no arms to bring them to Glinda, the good witch. But before that they had to fight with the Kalidahs, and then the giant spiders that were bigger than elephants with legs like trees. The Lion jumped on the biggest one and bit off its head."

"And Grandpa read all this to you?"

"But he said that I shouldn't be scared because the bad witch was melted. Why did she melt?"

"I think Dorothy poured water on her."

"But when we take a shower we don't melt," the boy said. "We're not bad witches."

"Maybe she melted because she was afraid of the Lion."

"That could be."

"But the Lion didn't have courage, so why would she be afraid of him?'

"Wouldn't you be afraid of a lion?"

"Yeah, I would. But I'm not a witch. Why did the Tin Man cut off his own head?" the boy asked.

"I don't know. Doesn't make sense, does it? What were your favorite parts of the story?"

"I liked when the house landed on the first witch, who was also bad. I didn't like when the Tin Man chopped off the heads of forty wolves. That was scary, but he killed them, so that was good."

"Killing isn't always good," his dad said.

"But the wolves were attacking them. And then the trees attacked them, and bees attacked them, and the monkeys attacked them and the spiders and the monsters. There was a lot of fighting."

"Maybe Grandpa shouldn't have read you the whole story."

"I liked it. I just don't want to see a Kalidah or the bad witches."

"The bad witches are gone, aren't they? And the Kalidahs aren't real, that's just make-believe."

"Maybe we can see them at the zoo."

"We could look for them, but I don't think they're there. It's just a story. I don't even know what a Kalidah looks like."

"I do. Their heads are tigers, and their bodies are bears, and their claws could cut you in half with one swipe."

"That's ... really something. Grandpa sure told you some story."

"And the Wizard wasn't really a wizard, he was just a man who pretended to be a wizard, and he put pins in the Scarecrow's head and told him they were brains, and he gave the Tin Man a toy heart, and told the Lion to drink green water that would give him courage."

"So, the Wizard was really fooling them," his dad said.

"But they believed him, they weren't so smart."

"Didn't he take Dorothy up in his balloon?"

"No, he just went by himself and Dorothy had to go see Glinda. And when she got there, Glinda said Dorothy didn't have to do everything she did, all she had to do was tap her shoes three times. She should have done that when she first got there."

"But then she wouldn't have met the Scarecrow, the Tin Man, or the Lion, and she wouldn't have had all those adventures."

"Yeah, but then I wouldn't have to think about the witch and the Kalidahs and the flying monkeys and the giant spiders."

"So, maybe next time you should ask Grandpa to read you *Winnie the Pooh*."

"Yeah. There are bees though."

"After *The Wizard of Oz*, you can't be scared of bees, can you?"

"Not small ones. But ones that are as big as hippos, maybe."

"I don't think there are any bees that big."

"You don't know, Dad. These are stories. Anything can happen."

LISTEN

Every day for fifty years, with just a few exceptions, John voiced whatever he was thinking to his wife Mary. If he read something interesting, he would tell her about it. If he heard a song he liked, or read a good book review, or saw something outrageous on the news, he would tell Mary what he thought. When they took walks, he talked about nature. When they took trips, he talked about history and architecture. When they went shopping, he talked about food. John loved to talk. When they watched TV, he commented on the characters and often predicted the plot twists. When they saw a movie, he always had an opinion of what they had seen.

But did Mary love to listen?

She certainly had fifty years' worth of opportunities. She didn't play sports, so she didn't get a chance to hear what he had to say during his golf, tennis, and pick-up basketball games, though he described them in detail when he got home. She didn't like violence, so she didn't share his enthusiasm for gangster, horror, or zombie stories.

What Mary was, was patient. Tolerant. Calm. Non-combative. Humble. Demure.

John always told people he had married a saint. He praised the way she cared for others. He extolled her kindness, her selflessness, her sharing. He told anyone who would listen that he'd rather eat her cooking than dine at a Michelin-rated restaurant. He lived a very fulfilled life with no complaints about the partner he chose to share it with.

Had he known what others would find out after he left this world, he probably would have been shocked. That's because when his brother had asked Mary to speak at his funeral, Mary said, simply, "I wouldn't know what to say."

"Of course you would," her brother-in-law said. "Who knew him better than you? He had opinions about everything, and you heard all of them."

"Not really," Mary said. "John liked to talk, but I rarely listened."

"How is that possible?" he asked.

"We got along," Mary said. "That's all I know, and probably all I could say. He liked to talk, yes. But he didn't ask questions. He didn't want to know what I thought about the things he talked about. Had he done so, I would have had to listen. But I learned long ago how to tune out the chatter than came from John's mouth. I had plenty to think about, and that's what I did. I thought about the books I read, the movies we saw, the music I heard. Whatever my eyes saw, or my ears heard, or my mouth tasted, or my fingers touched, I thought about that. John had his own thoughts about all of that, of course, and he voiced those thoughts. It used to crowd my head, until I realized that if I just let him go on, his voice could become like elevator Muzak to me, a background hum, a buzz-like meditation mantra that allowed me to go deeper into my own thoughts. I really wouldn't know what to say about John that people wouldn't already know. I would much prefer to hear what others had to say."

"You mean to tell me," her brother-in-law asked, "that you tuned him out completely? For fifty years? He always told me you were his best companion, his closest confidante, the person he told everything. Now you're telling me you heard nothing? That what he said, for fifty years, went in one ear and out the other?"

"We had a strong marriage," Mary said. "We didn't need to listen to each other to love each other."

"Who was his favorite writer?"

"No idea."

"Did he prefer Billie Holiday or The Beatles?"

"Beats me."

"What was his drink of choice?"

"That one I know, because I'd pour him his Scotch before dinner."

"I'm flabbergasted, Mary. Really, I am. John would be, too, I'm sure."

"Don't be too sure. I think he knew."

"Knew that you didn't listen to anything he had to say? Knew that instead of the bond he felt between you there was a gap a mile wide? If he hadn't died, and heard this, it would have killed him."

"Nonsense," Mary said. "You're overreacting. No marriage is the same. We never argued. He never raised his voice, and neither did I. Our sex life was good, as was our marriage."

"You might as well have been deaf."

"Then I wouldn't have heard the things I heard outside of John's jabber. Why don't you think about what you would like to say about your brother, and I'll listen."

"What I have to say? We hardly spoke since we moved to different states."

"So, talk about growing up together. That would be nice."

"We fought a lot, Mary. I don't want to talk about that at his funeral."

"So, you're saying that you, too, have nothing to say. I find *that* strange."

"What about his friends? They'll talk about him."

"I'm sure they will."

"But you won't?"

"Oh, I'll talk *to* him, in my own way. Just not at his funeral. What we had isn't something I'd want to share."

"But you just did, with me."

"Yes, I did. And what I heard was that you, who grew up in the same house with John, have nothing to say about him. That makes me sad."

"And you? You don't even know what he had to say."

"Guess that's why we're here now. To honor a man we both loved. In our own way."

The church was packed with people who came to pay their respects and to listen to those who stood up to tell stories about John. His golfing buddies spoke of what a crummy golfer he was, his tennis partner joked about his lousy serve, his poker cronies laughed at all the tells he displayed, his business associates talked about how much John admired Mary. One after another of his friends and acquaintances related something new, something funny, something touching about John. It was a lovely way to say goodbye to a good and decent man who liked to talk. And whose wife preferred not to listen, for they had had, what most would have called, a perfect marriage.

ONCE UPON A TIME

"Now that you're learning to read," Aunt Alice said, "you'll soon be able to take a book to bed with you and read it all by yourself."

"Will you be dead when I'm starting to read?" her niece asked.

"I sure hope not," she said.

"When will you be dead?"

It was a question Alice had been asking herself ever since she dreamed of her demise in a car accident when she was eighteen—sixty years ago. It was not just a disturbing dream, but a recurring one, and it had altered the course of her life.

After her tenth birthday, her father had brought her to the hospital where he worked, so she could see firsthand what a surgeon did. Her father's father had done the same with him, and he was continuing the family's tradition. Her mother read her stories as a child that extolled the virtues and nobility of the medical profession. It was a given that Alice would become a doctor, hopefully a surgeon or, if she wasn't up to cutting into living bone and tissue, then a researcher who might one day discover the cure for a deadly disease.

Then came the death dream, the one that repeated itself every few months for a year. That convinced her it was more a prophecy than a dream. She believed that she was going to die an early death and so decided to forego the arduous path to becoming a surgeon. Instead, she would live as much in the moment as she could, to take in all that life had to offer. Because her parents could afford it, she would take advantage of their largesse to explore the world, continent by continent. Instead of medical school, she studied photography and took writing courses, and learned to live the life of a freelancer.

"Grandma said you never wanted to have children." The child's words brought her back.

"Oh, that's my sister being jealous," Aunt Alice said with a laugh. "She had enough children for the two of us."

"Don't you like children?"

"Of course," Alice said. "And I like you most of all."

"I know that. Can you tell me a story about when you were a girl?"

"I like to think that even as old as I am, and I'm pretty old, I'm still a girl at heart. Where should I begin?"

"Anywhere."

"Well, my father—your great-grandfather—was a doctor, just like your grandmother and your mother. He wanted me to be a doctor, too, but I didn't have the patience to stay in school for so long. I wanted to travel and see the world."

"That's what I want, too," said the girl.

"And maybe you will, though the world is a very different place now than it was when I was young. Back then, I could get on a plane and fly anywhere I wanted, and I did. And wherever I went, there were a lot of young men who wanted to take me out. So, I let them—but only if I liked them."

"Did any of them want to marry you?"

"Oh, a few did. But I didn't want to settle down. I was what you'd call a free spirit. I'd spend time in different cities, in different countries, learn to speak a little Spanish or French, Russian or Japanese, but I was just too restless to want to stay in one place. If I married, I would have had to live wherever my husband lived. I wouldn't have lived the life I did."

"Are you sorry you didn't?"

"Not in the least. I got to see a million flamingoes all together in a lake in Tanzania, wild elephants and giraffes and rhinos in Kenya, men who dressed as women with heavy makeup on their faces in India, people who lived on houseboats in Kashmir, women who carried great sacks of wet salt on their heads in Columbia. I climbed Mt. Kilimanjaro and made it to the base camp of Mt. Everest. I saw an elephant paint a picture in Thailand, and a man who stuck his head inside an alligator's mouth in the Florida Everglades. I took pictures of men who swallowed fire and swords in Mexico City, and butchers who painted the heads of pigs orange in Kathmandu. I ran with the bulls in Spain and ran away from thieves in Peru. I saw Lenin's tomb in Moscow, visited the Ajanta caves, took a raft down the Colorado River in the Grand Canyon where I washed my hair under the Havasu Falls. I traveled with a camel caravan in the Sahara Desert, spent New Year's Eve in Timbuktu, spent weeks photographing a small circus in Guatemala. I even had a romance with a famous writer who lived in Vermont, but even your grandma doesn't know about that."

"How come you didn't want to be a doctor?"

"Is that what you want to be?"

"I think I want to be a ballerina."

"That takes more dedication than even being a doctor. There aren't many ballerinas these days."

"Maybe I could be a sword swallower."

"That's more like it. Yuck!"

"Or a lion tamer."

"Now you're thinking. Use your imagination. You can be anything you like. As long as you keep some of your dreams a secret."

"Do you have many secrets?"

"I sure do, honey."

"Daddy doesn't like it when I keep secrets."

"Then don't tell him you have them."

"You're funny, Aunt Alice."

She had had an exciting life. Her memoir cataloguing her travels was shortlisted for a National Book Award. She was a popular speaker at ashrams and wellness centers. Her eighteen-minute TED talk about living footloose and fancy free had four million downloads. But now, as she was approaching eighty, she began to have that dream again. The dream that had turned her life in another direction. The dream that turned out not to be prophetic, but just a dream, newly triggered by her young niece's innocent question: Would she be alive in the few months it would take for the girl to be able to read on her own?

There had been no death by car crash. There had been no life of healing the sick and raising a family. And, she was certain, there had been no mistake about her road less taken. All because, once upon a time, very long ago, she didn't believe there would even be a road to take.

NAKED PICTURES

When Martin Sanger turned forty, he decided it was time to get married. He didn't live a rocking bachelor's life; never even wanted to be a bachelor. It was just what Fate had in store for him—to live a lonely life, alone. To fantasize what married life might be. It was his bad luck to be shy and awkward; to be uncertain of what to say; to be bad at small talk, and worse, at talk that mattered. Though the people he knew didn't think of him this way, he thought of himself as one of life's losers.

The idea of having a wife appealed to him, even though he had no woman in mind. Among the cubicles on the floor where he worked, he had functioning, friendly relationships with six women. Three were married, one was engaged, the other two were gay. He couldn't bring himself to ask any of them if they had friends who were looking to settle down. But he had the Internet.

When he Googled "Mail-Order Brides," he found a YouTube documentary, a shopper's guide, and a bunch of websites that listed women from all over the world looking for husbands. He could choose from Eastern Europeans, Asians, Latinos, Africans, even some from New Guinea. He could see photos of these women, be in touch with them via social media, and have video chats. It seemed a bit overwhelming to Martin, who would have preferred to skim through a printed catalog, choose a woman from each continent, and narrow it down from there. That was the way it used to be, according to what he read on Wikipedia, but times had changed. Today, women also took an active role in choosing their future mates.

What Martin felt he needed to do was spruce up before going online to meet someone who most likely didn't speak his language. Appearance was important and Martin knew he could use some help. He went to a hair stylist and spent ninety dollars getting his hair cut, triple what he usually paid. He went to the men's department at Nordstrom's and bought a few silk and linen shirts, a cashmere sports jacket, and two pairs of pants. He treated himself to a day spa and got a facial and an herbal wrap, things he had never done before. It was all to boost his confidence, so that he could choose the right women to meet online and see if any of them wanted to get to know him.

To his surprise, because he had never done anything like this before, he discovered that he was a highly desirable male. Maybe that had to do with the fact that he presented himself as a homeowner, with a new car, and a decent bank account. But even snazzed up, he didn't come across as what one would call a "handsome" man, but in the questionnaire he filled out, it was apparent that if this was really him, he seemed like a guy that a young, attractive woman could control. The women who put themselves out there knew that it was mostly older, lonely men who were looking for wives who could cook and cuddle; just as they were looking for sugar daddies who could buy them things and make them materially secure. Love had little to do with this, but it wasn't out of the question. Anything was possible.

Of all the women who responded to Martin's profile, he narrowed it down to three: one each from Poland, the Philippines, and Thailand. The Pole had the fullest figure, the Filipina looked the most wholesome, but the Thai woman's vibe that came through her photo gave him an erection. Her name was Lamai. She was 31, with long black hair, a warm smile, and a face that matched her name, which meant gentle and caring. That was all Martin wanted from a match made online, a gentle, caring woman …. who also gave him an erection.

They got to know each other through video visits. Lamai couldn't speak English, and Martin knew no Thai, but they managed because Lamai's friend, Anong, acted as an interpreter. Anong was as attractive as Lamai, but Martin wasn't aroused by her, so even though he was talking via Zoom to two women, he only had eyes for one. There was talk, naturally, of what Martin had to offer to his potential bride. Martin was upfront that he was willing to share all that he had if it worked out between them. But would Martin agree to Lamai's one condition?

"And what condition is that?" Martin asked.

It had to do with sex, Anong explained. Lamai wanted to find a man who loved and cared for her because of who she was, and not because he was looking for a sex partner. Lamai's condition was that if she came to live with Martin, they would not have sex for the first six months.

"I can accept that," Martin said. "Does that mean she would need her own room? Or could we share a bedroom, but keep it respectful?"

Anong explained Martin's question to Lamai, and Lamai said that sharing a room would be acceptable. She said that since they didn't speak each other's languages, and since Anong wouldn't be around to translate (except via Zoom), they could learn to be close but not intimate for six months, and then they would know if they were meant to be with each other.

Martin offered to send Lamai a thousand dollars a month, and one year after they connected, Lamai got her visa and flew to the U.S. to meet Martin. She was everything he had hoped for from their meetings-at-a-distance, and more. More beautiful, more friendly, more amazing that she would be interested in him. Both of them were shy, but since they had made a pact not to rush into things right away, that worked to their benefit.

Martin took his two-week vacation time when Lamai arrived and they were able to spend that time together, exploring the city, going to the theater, taking a boat ride, and shopping. Lamai didn't waste any time refurnishing Martin's house, and she got along well with his dog. She didn't find their sleeping arrangement awkward, though Martin had to do his best acting to not show his frustration. Especially since Lamai wasn't shy about sleeping naked. She had a beautiful, unblemished body, with firm breasts and buttocks, a flat stomach, and shapely arms and legs. Martin was relieved that she wasn't a ladyboy, but a real woman, and he couldn't believe that such a woman had come to share his bed. He also couldn't believe that he had promised not to touch her for six excruciating months.

There was no way he could sleep without pajamas, because he needed to hide the small, but solid, protrusion between his legs. His only hope was that she would make the first move and they would consummate their relationship. But Lamai didn't seem bothered or frustrated by their situation and fell quickly to sleep each night. Martin, on the other hand, stayed awake, looking at her, for hours. He never touched her, but he did turn the blanket down to stare at her body, and to take pictures.

This might have seemed perverse, a violation of Lamai's person, but Martin had no intention of doing anything other than look at the pictures, especially when he returned to work, sitting in his cubicle, wondering what she was doing while he was gone. And when he pulled up the photos on his phone, he found himself so aroused that he would run to the men's room to relieve himself.

In the evening, Lamai prepared special Thai dishes that added to the joy of having her there. They would eat, drink, watch TV, and go online to see Anong, who translated what each wanted to tell the other. It was all working out the way each had hoped it would. And then, one day, Lamai picked up Martin's ringing phone to bring it to him in the bathroom, when she accidentally touched the photo app and saw her naked, sleeping body. She quickly scrolled through all the other photos Martin had taken of her and put the phone down, to think about what he had done.

Martin had been kind and generous to her. He had not made any demands; he had not forced himself on her; he had respected their agreement and she respected him for that. But these pictures? It felt like he was stealing something from her. It felt dark, and wrong, and very much like rape. But because of their language difficulties, she didn't want to make a scene and start screaming at him. She knew she would have to wait until they connected with Anong, and then she would confront him.

That night, when they both went to bed, Lamai put one arm over her head and curved her body in a seductive position, faking sleep. Martin waited until he was sure she was sleeping before he took his phone, pulled down the bedsheet, and snapped her photo. Lamai didn't move until Martin left the bed to go to the bathroom. Within a few minutes, she got up quietly and slightly pushed open the bathroom door, where Martin was sitting on the toilet masturbating, phone in one hand, looking at the photo he had just taken. Lamai thought of opening the door to let him see that she knew what he was doing, and what he had done. But she didn't. She went back to bed and faked sleep again.

When Martin fell asleep and began to snore, she got up, found his phone, and deleted all the pictures he had taken of her.

At work the next day, Martin took a break to find a stall, so he could look at his pictures and pleasure himself. When none of the pictures were there, he panicked. What had he done to accidentally delete them all? he wondered. This was terrible. It never occurred to him that it was Lamai.

But he found out soon enough, when he returned home, and they hooked up with Anong. Lamai had already told her about the pictures and Martin walked into an inquisition.

"Why?" Anong asked Martin. "She wants to know why you did such a thing?"

Martin didn't know what to say. He had been caught, he had no excuse, it was wrong, and he admitted so. "But it's been very difficult for me," he told Anong, who translated what he said to Lamai. "Every night, she sleeps without clothes, her body is so beautiful, and I can't express myself to her. I agreed not to have sex with her, but for weeks my balls hurt so bad from a constant erection that I began to walk funny. The only relief I was able to get was from masturbation. So, I took pictures of her asleep, and masturbated to them, imagining what it would be like one day when she's awake, and the time is right for us to do it."

Martin said all of this looking at Lamai, crying from embarrassment and a sense of his wrongdoing, knowing that he had hurt her.

"How many pictures were there?" Anong asked. "Lamai said there were a lot."

"One for every night since she's been here," Martin admitted.

"She wants to know if you jerked off every night?"

"I have," Martin said, feeling humiliated. He didn't want to lie about it.

"You drove him crazy," Anong said to Lamai.

"Yes, the poor man," Lamai said. And then the two women began to laugh.

Martin felt confused. His face burned, knowing that they were laughing at him, feeling sorry for him. He was sure that she would pack up and leave the next day.

"She wants you to know that she forgives you," Anong said. "But you must promise, no more pictures."

"No, none, I promise," Martin said, totally relieved. Was it possible that she was so understanding?

"She says she has a new condition," Anong said.

"Anything," Martin said.

"If you keep your promise, no more pictures, she will have sex with you in two weeks."

Martin couldn't believe what he was hearing. Two weeks? That might seem like an eternity, but knowing what was to come, at least he had something to look forward to. He didn't know what she would think of him when the time finally came, but for now, he was the happiest he had ever been.

Or so he thought. For when the time came and Lamai lay naked in bed, wide awake with open arms, summoning him to seal their union, Martin struggled to make it work. He had spent all these months having sex with her photos, able to satisfy himself by himself, but now that it was showtime, he couldn't arouse himself sufficiently to consummate their relationship. His happiness turned to tears of anxiety, and once again he feared she would leave him.

But Lamai wasn't going anywhere. Her life was comfortable the way it was, and if it would take more time and patience to coordinate Martin's head with the lower half of his body, that was fine with her.

"I'm so ashamed," Martin said, sitting on the edge of the bed.

"Don't be," Lamai said in the little English she could muster, as she stretched herself in a sexy pose. "Get your phone. We'll make this work."

COUNTING

All his life, ever since he knew how, Hugh Stratton counted. He counted out loud the fifty pushups he did each morning, the twenty leg-ups, the thirty sit-ups. He counted each step when he walked up and down his stairs. He counted how many steps it took to walk around his block. He counted how many strokes it took to swim a lap in his pool, over and over, with the numbers varying only slightly. He counted how many strokes he made on his beard as he talked on the phone. He counted how many sips he took of his morning coffee; how many times he stirred his hot cereal as it cooked; how many pieces of rope licorice he cut to make them bite size; how many gum chews he did per minute. He counted fallen leaves as he swept his patio. He counted the spines of books on his bookshelves. He counted squares in crossword puzzles, rails in railings. He counted clouds. He counted his sneezes. He would have counted raindrops during a spring rain if he could.

He never thought anything of all his counting until his friend Tom called him an obsessive compulsive. "You know you have OCD," Tom said.

"Why do you say that?" Hugh asked.

"Because you're an addict. You can't help yourself."

"And what is my addiction?" Hugh asked.

"You're a counter."

"You only know this because I told you about it," Hugh said.

"And ever since you did, I've been watching you. I can see your lips moving, number by number, whenever we're doing something. You count everything, don't you?"

"So, what if I do?"

"I'm just saying, that's all."

"You're saying that I need help?"

"Didn't say that," Tom said.

"What are you saying then?"

"Nothing. Just an observation."

"And should I count that against you?" Hugh asked.

"Ha. Funny. Okay, drop it. I didn't mean anything by it."

But Hugh couldn't drop it. Tom wasn't criticizing him, just naming his compulsion. And it was true—it was. But was it bad? How neurotic was he? Was it something he should learn how to undo?

Tom only knew the half of it. Hugh never told him how he counted himself to sleep. How he counted his shaving strokes. How he counted the strokes it took to jerk off, or to bring his wife to orgasm. And he certainly never told Tom how often he counted just for the sake of counting.

Numbers didn't fascinate him the way they might a mathematician. To him, they were what they were, a series of progressions. He had studied Spanish and French in high school and college and sometimes counted in those languages, but it got tricky when he was counting past fifty, so he mostly kept to English.

One of his favorite ditties was the Bottles of Beer, counting down from a hundred bottles of beer on the wall, and when one fell, it would be ninety-nine bottles, all the way down to no more bottles of beer on the wall. He often recited this when he was driving, that is, when he was not engaged in counting how many Teslas or Priuses he saw, or how many green lights he drove through before one turned red.

"I've been thinking," his friend Tom said a few weeks later. "It's too bad you're not a gambler, because you could make a killing in Vegas counting cards."

"That's a different kind of counting," Hugh said. "That has to do with memorization. That's not what I do. I just count."

"There's got to be some way to put what you do to use. Ever go to the racetrack?"

"Once or twice."

"What if you counted the number of times a horse galloped? Maybe figure out what horse runs best with the least or most strides?"

"They move too fast."

"Yeah, but if you tape it and slow it down, you could count them."

"You're a schemer, aren't you, Tom? Trying to figure out some way to cheat the system."

"Maybe you could count how many steps a bank guard takes from his car to the bank, figure out a way to get in and out before he pulls his weapon."

"There's an easier way than counting," Hugh laughed. "It's called using a watch. And since when did you go from being a car dealer to a bank robber?"

"I'm just thinking out loud, is all. There must be some use you could put to your obsession. You should have been an accountant."

"I'm perfectly happy with what I do."

"Yeah, but how does counting fit in with grading papers and teaching American history to high school juniors and seniors?"

"One has nothing to do with the other, so why try to correlate the two?"

"You know those contests, where you win a prize if you can guess the number of pennies in a jar? What if you ..."

"I have no desire to count a jar full of pennies."

"I'll think of something," Tom said.

"You do that," Hugh laughed. "I just hope you're not losing sleep over this."

Hugh got a kick out of his friend's attempts to put his counting to some use, but he knew what he did was of little value and was probably a habit worth trying to break. It wasn't that he felt trapped with his counting, because he didn't. But now that he told Tom about it, Tom would probably tell others, and it would just get awkward in time.

Neither Tom nor Hugh could have imagined how Hugh's obsession might fit in with his teaching, but it did on the day that a disgruntled, unbalanced senior, who had taken Hugh's history class the previous semester, decided to borrow his father's pistol and make a name for himself. Hugh was in class, teaching, when he heard the shots coming from the hallway. Then the screaming and the sounds of running. "Everyone down!" Hugh commanded. "Under your desks." He moved towards the door, to try and block it with his desk, but didn't make it in time. The shooter had already come into his class.

"I'm sorry Mr. Stratton," he said, his handgun pointed in front of him. "History is bullshit."

"History gets repeated," Hugh said, recognizing the student but not remembering his name. "Others have done what you're doing. It never ends well."

One of the students under a desk near the door thought he'd be a hero and made a move toward the shooter, who turned and pulled the trigger, sending a bullet into his arm. The student fell backwards, and Hugh went towards the shooter.

"That's enough," he said calmly. "You've done enough damage. Now, give me the gun."

The shooter pointed his gun at his former teacher, but Hugh didn't flinch. The shooter pulled the trigger.

Click. The barrel was empty.

Hugh grabbed the gun, the shooter tried to pull away, but Hugh was able to overpower him. "It will be all right now," he said, both to the shooter and to the students in the room. "It's over now."

Word soon spread of Mr. Stratton's heroics, how he stood up to the shooter and walked towards him, facing certain death. But Hugh knew he wasn't a hero. He had recognized that the gun pointed at him was a Ruger blued SP 101, that had a five-round capacity. It was the same small frame gun he had bought for his wife to protect herself from an intruder. He had counted four shots when the shooter entered his classroom. The fifth wounded one of his students. He knew the gun was empty. It wasn't an act of foolish bravery, just his counting compulsion that had brought the incident to an end.

That wasn't the way it was reported on the news that evening and in the newspapers the following day. Hugh Stratton had put his obsession to good use. He didn't talk about his counting, though both his wife and Tom had figured it out.

"Were you scared?" his wife asked that night.

"Not after the fifth shot," Hugh said. "I was worried about the student he shot and just wanted to end it, so he could get help."

"What if the chamber wasn't empty? What if it was a six-round pistol?"

"I recognized it. It was just luck that I knew what it was."

"Well, I'll no longer tease you when you count every step when we walk."

When the phone stopped ringing, and Hugh said all he could about the incident, they settled in to watch TV.

"Popcorn tonight?" Hugh asked his wife.

"Why not?" she said. "Mr. Hero."

Hugh went upstairs to the kitchen to measure the kernels into the silicone popper he had bought online, then put it in the microwave and set it for four minutes, 240 seconds which he would count once he pressed the Popcorn key at the top left on the panel. But he accidentally hit the key below it, which was Level Ten, the highest power. When his wife called to him, he went downstairs to their TV room to see what she wanted. She was searching through their watch list on Netflix, trying to decide what they might watch. He smiled at her as he continued counting down the seconds. He still needed to get the popcorn bowl ready, take out the salt, and the potholders to grab the popper when it was done.

When his internal count reached 110, his wife asked him if he'd rather watch a movie or a documentary.

"What're the choices?" he asked.

She offered up a nature or a political documentary, or a Woody Allen or Charlie Kaufman film. Hugh ran each choice through his mind and said, "You choose. Surprise me."

But he was in for a much greater surprise as, at the two-and-a-half-minute mark, the corn kernels in the silicone popper overheated and erupted into flames. By the time Hugh got back to the kitchen and smelled the burning before he saw the fire, the microwave door had burst open, the dishtowels next to it fueled the fire, and half the kitchen was ablaze. It was that fast.

The extinguisher was under the sink, but it was too late to get to it. His wife came running up the stairs and saw him trying to put out the fire with a towel he had grabbed from the bathroom, but it only served to fan the flames.

"Call 911!" he shouted.

The fire department responded within minutes and saved the house from burning down. But the kitchen and dining room were toast.

"How did this happen?" his wife asked. "This never happened before."

"You distracted me," Hugh said.

"And how did I do that?"

"You asked me to choose something to watch."

"And what has that to do with setting our house on fire?"

"I was timing the popper, counting down the seconds."

"And?"

"And I lost count."

DO *YOU* LIKE DONUTS?

At the children's cancer ward, Kojo Appiah found a dozen images of different Shopkins on the Internet and made copies to show four-year-old David for the in-hospital video show he produced. David was an out-patient who came in twice a week for his leukemia treatments. His mother gave him a new Shopkin after each treatment, and David already had quite a collection.

Kojo Appiah set up his video camera on a tripod, turned it on, and sat down in a chair by David's bed. "I heard you really know your Shopkins," he said in a slight British accent. "If I show you some, can you tell me their names?"

"Okay," little David said, looking at this strange, happy man. "What's your name again?"

"Kojo. It's an African name."

"It sounds funny. Like the gorilla that talks. We have that book."

"That's Koko. My other name is even funnier. It's Appiah." He said it as Ap-pee-a, because he knew it would make David smile, which it did.

"Is it really Pee-a?" David asked.

"It is."

"Do people make fun of your name?"

"Not really. Should they?"

"I think so. It's a really funny name. Pee-a."

Kojo held up a picture of a plastic strawberry with pursed lips.

"Strawberry Kiss," David said.

Kojo showed him a tube of lipstick.

"Lippy Lips."

"What about this one?"

"Kooky Cookie."

"Well, David, you don't even take time to think. You really know your Shopkins."

David recognized Apple Blossom, Pineapple Crush, Miss Mushy-Moo, Cheeky Chocolate, Roller Roller Blade, Frieda Fern, and Cherry Cherry.

"And what about this easy one?" Kojo asked.

"That's Dlish Donut."

"Yum," Kojo said. "Wish we had some now. Do you like donuts?"

"Yes," said David, thinking he meant did he like the Shopkin. Then he realized that Kojo was asking him about actual donuts. "No," he said, "Do *you* like donuts?" It was more like an accusation than a question.

Kojo was caught off guard. What kid didn't like donuts? "Well, sure," he said.

"I don't like donuts," David said, remembering the time at a three-year-old friend's party, when he bit into one and spit it out. "My mom says they're no good for you. Why do you like them?"

Kojo smiled weakly at the child, then at David's mother. "I …. guess I really don't like donuts," he said.

"But you said you did," David said.

"Some people like donuts," Kojo said. "Some only like certain kinds of donuts."

"If they're not good for you, then you shouldn't like them."

"You're right, I shouldn't. And I won't. And I don't. I mean …. shall we see who this is?" He held up a picture of a hamburger wearing a hat.

"I like fruit," David said.

"Fruit's good," Kojo said, finding one among his copies. "Know this one?"

"Posh Pear," David said.

When Kojo had enough for a three-minute video he told David that the next time he came to the hospital, he would be able to see himself on the television. Before he left the room, he apologized to David's mother for bringing up the donuts.

"Oh, that's fine," she said. "We've let him try them, but he doesn't care for them. Maybe it's the texture, though he does eat gluten free organic muffins."

Kojo made an ugh face and smiled. "Maybe next time I'll bring him one of those."

"That's very kind of you, but it isn't necessary. And thank you for taking an interest in David. I can see that he likes talking to you."

"Tell you the truth," Kojo said, "I haven't met a child like him before. He speaks in complete sentences, he has an incredible memory, he asks questions, and he's funny. I like being with him."

Kojo knew how the mothers of these children suffered and suspected that she thought he was just saying nice things about her son to cheer her up, but he meant what he said.

In the two years he had worked on the ward, he met many brave, sullen, compliant, or scared children of different ages and degrees of illness. He brought them small gifts of crayons and drawing pads, stickers, books, toy cars, flashlights, whatever the department bought with funds that were donated to entertain the children. He thought of the hardships of his own childhood in West Africa, where a new toy was as rare as a lunar eclipse, and he had to make do with hand-me-downs, rusty hoops that could be rolled with a stick, and worn-out soccer balls that were always half inflated.

He had come to America to study nursing and found that he had an affinity for working with vulnerable children. They mostly seemed to accept their fate more than adults, who cursed God for their illnesses. When the Corona virus broke out, he was told that if he left the country he wouldn't be allowed back in until the virus had subsided and a vaccine was in place, so he put off any plans to see his parents and friends and put all his energy into bringing smiles to children with cancer.

Little David lifted his spirits. He laughed as he drove to his apartment that evening, thinking about how David had asked him about liking donuts and how David's mother had said he liked gluten free, organic, bland muffins. He made a note to find a donut shop that made sugar free donuts to bring with him the next time he saw David.

That next time was four days away, giving Kojo plenty of time to locate a bakery that had hundreds of five-star Yelp reviews for their donuts. On the morning of his afternoon visit with David to show him the Shopkins video, Kojo stood in a long line at the bakery. As most shops were either closed or had very few patrons, he figured these donuts must really be special, since a lot of people were willing to risk catching the virus to get them. Once he got to the counter and selected what he thought David might like, he hoped that David's mother would let him give them to David.

"You can try," David's mother said when Kojo walked into their room with a box of six freshly baked, sugar free donuts. One was glazed, another had sprinkles, and the others were chocolate, plain, or filled with custard or almond paste.

"So, David," Kojo said, as a nurse was beginning his treatment, "look what I brought you. Six different delicious donuts that your mom says is okay for you to taste."

David looked up from his bed, the chemo beginning to drip slowly into his arm, the bill of the baseball cap covering his bald head turned to the right of his forehead, and saw his mother nod. "But I don't like donuts," he said.

"That's because you haven't tried these," Kojo said.

David looked into the box, trying to decide which to choose. Kojo assumed he'd go for the one with the colorful sprinkles, but David chose the custard-filled one.

"How come it doesn't have a hole? Is this a donut?"

"I think so, but it has something inside where the hole would be."

David hesitated, then picked it up and bit into it. Kojo was smiling, sure he would like it.

"Yuck," David said, spitting it out. "It's mushy."

"That's all right, honey," his mother said. "That's why Kojo brought different ones. You can try another if you like."

"I don't think so," David said, wiping his tongue on the back of his hand.

"How about just a bite of the chocolate one?" Kojo suggested.

David wasn't sure, but he felt sorry for Kojo and didn't want to disappoint him. So, he took a bite of the chocolate donut and spit it out before he swallowed any of it.

"I told you," David said. "It's disgusting." 'Disgusting' was a new word that he had picked up from a Looney Tunes cartoon.

"Well, there are four others you can try," Kojo said. "I'll leave them with you, and maybe you can take them home and try them when you're feeling better."

"I feel okay," David said.

Kojo smiled at him, turned on the television, and found the in-hospital channel. Up came David on the monitor, naming the Shopkins.

"I didn't know the Hamburger one," David said. It was the only one he had missed.

"Maybe it's Hammy Hamburger," Kojo said.

"No, that's not it. I think it's Cheezey B."

"You know, I think you're right."

David smiled. "I just forgot it."

"You probably forget more than I remember," Kojo said.

A few weeks later, Kojo's temperature was too high to allow him back into the cancer ward, even though he felt fine. But the hospital was very strict about anyone coming in if they hadn't been tested for the virus and showed any signs of a fever. Kojo, like all the hospital employees, got tested weekly, and this time, he tested positive. He had been overly cautious ever since the virus appeared; he wore the proper protective clothing, always put on a mask, a face shield, washed his hands after each visit to a child, used hand sanitizer, surgical gloves, and bootie wraps around his shoes. He stayed in his apartment all the time, only venturing out to go to work or buy food. Still, the virus got him. And made him sick.

When David's mother heard about Kojo, she tried to keep the news from David, but the boy asked about him, and she told him that he wasn't feeling well.

"Can we visit him?" David asked.

"I'm not sure, honey," she said. "He may be in quarantine."

"What's that?"

"It means he could be contagious. He could infect other people if they get close to him."

David thought about it, then took his drawing pad and began drawing different Shopkins. When he covered the page, he asked his mother how to spell Kojo and wrote the four letters at the top, printing his name, with a backward D, at the bottom.

"Can you give this to Kojo?" he asked his mother.

"Let's give it to the nurse to give to him."

"Okay, maybe it will make him feel better."

"I think it will," his mother said.

Being sick was something David understood. That's why he was being treated at the hospital, along with all the other children who were there. He'd seen some get better and some get worse. This was what life was for him.

Kojo Appiah was on a ventilator when the nurse entered his isolated room. He was still conscious and gave a thumbs up when she showed him David's drawing, though it was heartbreaking to see how weak her African coworker was.

When she returned to David's room, he looked at her sad face and asked if Kojo liked his drawing.

"He did, very much. He went like this," she said, pointing her thumb up.

"Is he going to die?"

"I hope not," the nurse said.

But David's mother knew that Kojo Appiah would not be visiting her son again. "He might not make it," she said softly. She and David had had conversations about the fragility of life. Death, she had told him, was when very sick people go to a better place, where their hair grows back, and they don't have to get any more needle 'pokies' and they feel fine.

"He shouldn't have eaten donuts," David said, starting to draw another picture.

"Guess not," his mother said, beginning to cry. She couldn't help wondering if Kojo might have gotten infected at the bakery where he bought the donuts.

"Don't cry, Mom," David said, drawing an Octonaut pod. "He just has to stop eating donuts, that's all."

Doing her best to suppress her tears, his mother said, "Of course, honey. That's all."

DOG

Between San Francisco and Palo Alto, in the small city of San Carlos, a weathered, bearded man pulls a four-wheeled four cubic foot garden dump cart through the streets near the children's park and surrounding churches. In the cushioned bed of the cart lay his old, crippled dog, part Irish wolfhound, part German shepherd. The kids at the park come running when they pass. They think it's funny that the man pulls the dog in the cart.

"What's his name?" a child asks.

"Dog," the man says.

"That's a funny name," another child says. "Can we pet him?"

"No."

"Is he sick?"

The man keeps moving. On Laurel, he finds an empty table outside The Broiler Express and sits down. He doesn't need to order the vegetable breakfast burrito and coffee because he's a regular. They know what he wants. When the food comes, they also bring leftover meats for the dog. When he finishes his breakfast, the man walks down the street looking at all the shops geared to children: a bookstore, a paint & clay store, a shoe store, a clothes store, and Diddams, the large toy and candy store. The man has no children. His dog was once a child to him, but now he's more an equal, his sole companion.

The man knows Dog doesn't have much life left. He has to carry him from the cart to the street for the dog to relieve himself. Dog weighs ninety pounds and is not easy to lift. The vet said it was time to put him down, but that was a year ago, when the incident happened. The man can't bring himself to say goodbye.

Because it's Sunday, the street is closed to traffic so the farmers can sell their produce. They all know the man and his dog and as he walks through the outdoor market, they fill the cart with fruits and vegetables. The man, and the dog, appreciate their charity. Neither say anything, though Dog wags his tail.

When they reach San Carlos Ave. the man stops to polish an apple from the cart and breaks it in two. He shakes out the pits and gives half to Dog. There's a small park nearby and he walks there to sit on a bench to rest. Someone has left a newspaper that he picks up to read. The news, as usual, is disturbing. The man has no patience and no desire to find out how bad things are. The sky is already orange from the wildfires, that's enough.

The dog looks sad. He knows the look and apologizes to the dog. He doesn't want to make things worse for his companion. Still, it's hard to smile when each day is a struggle.

They are two miles from their tent. They have enough food to get them through the next few days, but the man is tired. He doesn't know how much longer he can do this, even though the people are nice to them. He knows they feel sorry for them, but pity is better than antipathy.

The man once had a name, a title, an expense account. He lived nicely in San Francisco, and then in Palo Alto. This was before Dog. It was Dog who found him, seven years ago, when the man was sleeping on a park bench in San Carlos. Dog had no collar, no tags, and smelled like he had been roaming for weeks or months. The man recognized a fellow traveler, called him "Dog," and they adopted each other. That's when the man got a tent, to make a home for the two of them.

Other than the man and the crazy person, only the vet knows what happened to Dog. It was one of those blink-of-the-eye, life-on-the-streets moments when all the man could do was rush to be by Dog's side, as he lay on the ground bleeding. The man had been inside their tent when he heard Dog bark. Then he heard the crazy person bark back and when the man stuck his head out, he saw the crazy person waving a hunting knife at Dog.

"Calm down," the man said, "he's not going to hurt you."

"You bet he won't," the crazy person said and stabbed Dog near his tailbone, cutting the nerves between his lower back and hind leg. The crazy person grabbed his shopping cart full of his belongings and ran away.

The man put Dog in his wagon and brought him to the vet. The vet said Dog would never walk again and should be put down. The man told him he wanted to keep Dog alive.

The man had coped the best he could being homeless but living in the streets meant having to deal with the mentally ill, and there was not much he could do about that. Dog certainly didn't deserve such a pointless attack, and there was no sense going after the perpetrator. If the man saw the crazy person again, he would let the police know, but he wouldn't go out of his way to find him. There were plenty of crazies living in tents and cardboard boxes in San Carlos, San Mateo,

Redwood City, and all over the Bay area. Dogs helped keep such people away, but not always. And not this time.

For seven years, the man slept with his arm around Dog. They managed to keep each other's spirits up, even when the nights got cold or the days got smokey. Dog was smaller than the average wolfhound, but bigger than a shepherd. He had a stoic personality and seemed to understand that the man needed him. But the stabbing took its toll and being paralyzed led to a decline in his health. The man could see that Dog's decline was irreversible.

The man pulls the wagon towards the children's park. The older children are in school, but the little ones are with their nannies being pushed on the swings, sliding down the slides, playing in the sandbox. This time, the man opens the short metal gate and enters the park. Some of the braver children come running towards them, wanting to take a closer look at the dog in the wagon.

"Can I pet him?" one four-year-old asks.

The man says yes.

The boy puts out his hand and Dog licks it.

Another child comes to pet Dog's body. And another shows no fear and pets Dog's head.

"Why is he in the wagon?" a child asks.

"He's old," the man says. "He can't walk."

Dog's tail is wagging. He's happy to be with the children. The man smiles at the children and winks at Dog. He makes Dog a promise that he will bring him back here for as long as he lives.

THE WORLD'S GREATEST STORIES

Christopher Walter Donnaggle sat at his computer trying to come up with a good name for his latest hero. He looked up at the photos on his wall but rejected the names of his family and friends because he had already used them in previous stories. He thought about politicians, past and present, and Ulysses struck him as a good name. Warren, too. And Dwight. Three names, maybe for the next three stories.

He was a writer on fire; a writer who never suffered from writer's block. His file drawers were filled with his stories. None had been published, but that didn't matter, because Christopher Walter Donnaggle was way ahead of his time. He was confidant because he knew a good story when he read one, and he knew that the stories he wrote were as good as any he had ever read. He was sure that his stories would one day rank among the greatest stories ever written.

It wasn't that he had never tried to publish. He wrote his first story when he was fifteen and was encouraged by his English teacher to submit it to the student literary magazine. It wasn't used because the editor was a senior and believed sophomores should learn a little humility before seeing their names in print. By the time Christopher was a senior, he had written twenty stories, none of them ever again submitted to the literary magazine. One of them, though, he sent to *The New Yorker* and got back a standard, unsigned letter of rejection. That was around the time he read *Martin Eden* by Jack London and got the insight and understanding he needed to turn away from submitting his work, but not to stop writing. He loved to write, and he loved to read about writing. He knew Hemingway's iceberg theory, Elmore Leonard's ten rules (his favorite was the tenth: "Try to leave out the part that readers tend to skip"), and agreed with Willa Cather that most of the basic material a writer works with is acquired by the age of fifteen. He shared the first half of Winston Churchill's comment about writing being an adventure: "To begin with, it is a toy and an amusement. Then it becomes a mistress, then it becomes a master, then it becomes a tyrant." He remained at the "mistress" stage and didn't think it would ever go further than that. For him, the act of writing was similar to pulling weeds from one's garden. No one saw what you did, but you pleased yourself by making the garden look good.

Though he had read Maugham, Munro, Millhauser, Poe, Kafka, Murakami, Saunders, and hundreds of other short story writers, he had come to believe, like Disraeli, that when he wanted to read a good story, he'd write one. And then another. And another.

He never ran out of ideas. He found them from newspapers, reality TV, Ted Talks, YouTube lectures, history books, observing children playing, athletes competing, animals doing what they did to survive and dominate. He carried a notebook with him and a small tape recorder, so he could write down or record overheard dialogue or scenes he observed while riding a bus, jogging in the park, at the gym, the zoo, the museums, or at any of the various jobs he had taken to support his writing. Because he was so dedicated, he didn't pursue the higher education needed to become a doctor, lawyer, scientist, or programmer. Nor did he try to be anything he wasn't in the writing field, like a screenwriter, playwright, novelist, journalist or poet. His genre was the short story.

When he read about an African stowaway who fell to his death from an airplane, he imagined the circumstances that led to the African's desperate attempt to leave his country behind and then wrote a story about it. When he saw the wildlife exhibit of endangered species at the airport, he wrote a dozen stories about the ivory-billed woodpecker, the amur leopard, the Javan and black rhinos, the Cross River and mountain gorillas, the Yangtze giant softshell turtle, the Indochinese tiger, the Indian cheetah, the pangolin, and the Spix macaw. When he heard the President of the United States say he was taking an unapproved drug to prevent him from getting the COVID-19 virus, he listened to what the doctors from both parties said about it and wrote a story trying to be as even-handed as any objective writer should be. How could he ever run dry? Stories were everywhere.

Though he had never married, Christopher had experienced love, jealousy, envy, grief, even a broken heart, and he wrote stories about all of these emotions. When he worked as a custodian in a high school, he wrote about teenagers. As a bank teller for two years, he gathered stories about his fellow workers and the people who came to make their deposits and withdrawals. (He once was a victim of a bank robbery and got four good stories out of that). When he drove a UPS truck, he delivered the boxes to those who could afford to buy things and that always gave him new ideas. As an Uber driver he was handed stories like gifts from those he picked up, their tales far more valuable than tips or ratings.

He worked out a filing system so that when he wrote stories about racial tension or unrequited love or a political satire, he knew where to put them. Over thirty-five years, those drawers filled with individually labeled folders, one story to a folder. He looked at those files with pride, unconcerned that no one had read any of the stories he had written, confident that posterity would know who he was, and that shelves would one day be filled with volume after volume of his work. His four file cabinets—each with four deep drawers—were like J. D. Salinger's safe, filled with stories the great recluse had written and hidden until after his death.

Christopher gave a lot of thought as to where he should bestow his unpublished oeuvre. He wasn't interested in selling them to a university, like the one in Austin, Texas, and he didn't much care for the snobbery of the Ivy League libraries. He thought that, since he had written about such a wide range of subjects, they should go to the Library of Congress, for all the world to have access to them, to enjoy the worlds he had so ardently chronicled.

He called a journalist he knew and invited him to his home. He wanted to show what he had achieved over his lifetime, without letting him read any of his stories. Rather, he wanted an article that would describe Christopher's accomplishment so that the Library of Congress would accept his donation when the time came.

And when the end came for Christopher Warren Donnaggle, he went to his rest knowing that selections of his work would be read by scholars, critics, reviewers, and acclaimed masters of the short story, per the agreement he had negotiated with the Library of Congress. They normally didn't accept unpublished work, but Christopher had written *so many* stories, they felt it might have potential cultural (as well as literary) value. For his part, Christopher believed that once his work was recognized by such an august institution, his reputation would be secured, and he would become known as the world's greatest short story writer.

But that didn't happen.

Though Christopher had understood that short stories needed structure, strong plots, well-paced narratives, intriguing characters, interesting dialogue, some kind of action, ironies and epiphanies, suspense and conflict, the consensus among the readers who read the few dozen they each had been given was that they just weren't very good.

One of Christopher's favorite writers, George Orwell, had viewed writing as an exhaustive struggle, like a long bout with a painful illness. "One would never undertake such a thing if one were not driven by some demon." But that was where Christopher Warren Donnaggle had differed with Orwell. Writing was a joy, not a struggle. He had no demons that drove him.

And without demons, he would remain the world's greatest story writer to an audience of one. But that had been enough for him to have lived a very fulfilled life.

OTHER BOOKS
BY LAWRENCE GROBEL

THE NARCISSIST: Stories

26 stories that range from Africa and India to Bangkok and
Paris, from funeral parlors to cancer wards, from spoiled
Beverly Hills teenagers to stand-up comedy. There's a
giant spider, a child kidnapping, a cargo ship from hell,
and a carousel that takes you back in time. Something for
everyone!

CATCH A FALLEN STAR (a novel)

An insider's Hollywood like *The Player* but with thematic
elements of *Wonder Boys*. The story of an actor who fails
upward. As his private battles go public, he must deal with
deceitful friends, devious journalists, and cunning studio
heads.

BEGIN AGAIN FINNEGAN (a novel)

How far would you go to help your best friend?

That's the question journalist Devin Hunter faces when
movie star Adrian Kiel asks him to be his alibi to cover a possible murder. Devin's decision starts a chain of events that

spiral out of control as he tries to hold the pieces of his life together. It peels back the culture of celebrity to reveal the snake pit underneath.

THE BLACK EYES OF AKBAH (a novella)

After leaving Ghana, where they served for two years in the Peace Corps, Eric and Anika agree to travel together to Kenya and India to get to know each other better and see if they want to spend the rest of their lives together. They agree to work their way across the Indian Ocean on a cargo ship ominously called The Black Eyes of Akbah. The crew is a melting pot of all the indigenous peoples of the region. They leave Mombasa for Mumbai, but the chilling terror that happens along the way will change the way they see each other and the world they thought they knew. Oliver Stone compared this story to a cross between *The African Queen* and *Midnight Express*.

COMMANDO EX (a novella)

Commando Ex is a wild Australian hedonist racing across Africa on his Motoguzzi motorcycle, chasing thrills and adventure, living life to the max and flaunting what you can be if you're absolutely free. After all, "What's to lose? An army to grab you? A desk job to nail you? A mechanic to jail you? Chuck it. Change your name, change the game, steal on a boat and float all the way to foreign places." "So, keep up, speed along, trip flip and skip through the one life worth living, the fully explored, high geared unfeared not scared life of the Commando. Sight ... on!"

THE HUSTONS

When John Huston died at 81 on August 28, 1987, America lost a towering figure in movie history. The director of such classic films as *The Maltese Falcon, The Treasure of the Sierra Madre, The African Queen, Prizzi's Honor,* and *The Dead*, John Huston was at the center of a dynasty, with three generations of Oscar winners (Walter, John and Anjelica). Here, the complete story of this remarkable family is told. J.P. Donleavy named *The Hustons* the best book of the year and James A. Michener dubbed it a "Masterpiece." The *Hollywood Reporter* said it "Reads like a gutsy movie that might have been made by Huston himself."

CONVERSATIONS WITH CAPOTE

Six months after Truman Capote died in 1984, *Conversations with Capote* was published and reached the top of best-seller lists in both New York and San Francisco. *Parade* called it "An engrossing read. Bitchy, high-camp opinions... from a tiny terror who wore brass knuckles on his tongue." Said the *San Francisco Chronicle*, "All the rumors you ever heard about Capote are here... Refreshing... thoughtful and reflective."

CONVERSATIONS WITH BRANDO

Playboy named Lawrence Grobel "The Interviewer's Interviewer" for his uncanny ability to get America's greatest and most reclusive actor, Marlon Brando, to speak openly for the first time. When Grobel expanded the interview into a book, *American Cinematographer* said it "penetrates the complex nature of a very private man, probing his feelings on women and sex, Native Americans, corporate America and the FBI."

CONVERSATIONS WITH MICHENER

The conversations between James A. Michener and Lawrence Grobel took place over 17 years, right up until the last week of Michener's life. Michener was a true citizen of the world. He foresaw the future of countries as diverse as Afghanistan, Poland, Japan, Spain, Hungary, Mexico, Israel, and the U.S. His books—like *Hawaii, The Source, Iberia, Sayonara*, and *Tales of the South Pacific*—sold millions of copies and many were made into films or TV miniseries.

CONVERSATIONS WITH AVA GARDNER

These conversations with the femme fatale of *The Killers, Mogambo, The Barefoot Contessa, Show Boat*, and *Night of the Iguana*, and one of the world's great beauties, are startlingly candid. The reclusive actress opened up about her three volatile marriages to Mickey Rooney, Artie Shaw and Frank Sinatra. She tells about Howard Hughes' 15-year pursuit of her and reveals how George C. Scott was so crazily in love with her that he beat her up on three occasions and once stuck a broken bottle in her face. She talks about her tomboy childhood as a tobacco farmer's daughter in North Carolina; admits to her struggles with alcohol; and speaks intimately about the debilitating stroke she suffered toward the end of her life.

CONVERSATIONS WITH ROBERT EVANS

"I don't want to have a slow death," Robert Evans told Lawrence Grobel. "That's my fear. I've had a gun put in my mouth; a gun put at my temple. I've had a gun put on me five different times to talk, and not once have I ever talked." But talk is what Evans does in these conversations. As the head of Paramount Studios in the 1970s, Evans produced some of the most iconic movies of that era, including *Love Story, The Odd Couple, Paper Moon, True Grit, Catch 22, Chinatown*, and *The Godfather*. This book is eye-opening in its honesty and its finger-pointing.

AL PACINO in Conversation with Lawrence Grobel

For more than a quarter century, Al Pacino has spoken freely and deeply with Lawrence Grobel on subjects as diverse as childhood, acting, and fatherhood. Here are the complete conversations and shared observations between the actor and the writer; an intimate and revealing look at one of the most accomplished, and private, artists in the world.

"I WANT YOU IN MY MOVIE!"
My Acting Debut & Other Misadventures Filming Al Pacino's *Wilde Salome*

"Why *am* I doing this?" Al Pacino wondered a year into his personal movie about his obsession with *Salome*, Oscar Wilde's lyrical play, written in 1891. "No one saw *Looking for Richard*, who's going to want to see something about Oscar Wilde?" Grobel found the answer to that question and more when he joined the crew and followed the creative process of filmmaking from inception to completion.

THE ART OF THE INTERVIEW: Lessons from a Master of the Craft

Joyce Carol Oates called Lawrence Grobel "The Mozart of Interviewers." *Playboy* named him "The Interviewer's Interviewer." And J.P. Donleavy wrote, "Grobel is the most intelligent interviewer in the United States." Here, Grobel reveals the most memorable stories from his career. Taking us step-by-step through the interview process, from research and question writing to final editing, *The Art of the Interview* is a treat for journalists and culture vultures alike.

YOU, TALKING TO ME: 120 Lessons Learned Along the Celebrity Trail

The Art of the Interview was about how to talk to people. This one is about what the author learned from the people he talked to. The *Interview* book looked outward; this book looks inward, detailing what Grobel has learned from talking to some of the most fascinating people of our time.

SIGNING IN: 50 Celebrity Profiles

From 2005—2010 Lawrence Grobel wrote over 70 magazine articles about his encounters with some of the most famous people in the world. Each piece had only one caveat: to include at least a paragraph about something the celebrity had signed. So, Grobel built each portrait around a signed photo, poster, drawing, personal letter, or book inscription, many of which are shown in this engaging book.

ICONS

Profiles of fifteen internationally beloved stars: Jack Nicholson, Angelina Jolie, Halle Berry, Anthony Hopkins, Kim Basinger, Anthony Kiedis, Jodie Foster, Nicole Kidman, Meryl Streep, Gwyneth Paltrow, Cameron Diaz, Tom Waits, Penelope Cruz, Sharon Stone, and Robert De Niro.

YOU SHOW ME YOURS: A Memoir

A journey through the Looking Glass of American Culture from the post-War '50s, the sexually liberated '60s, the Civil Rights movement, the Peace Corps, Performance Art, and the "Me Decade." Diane Keaton calls this book "Profoundly entertaining and totally INSANE!" It's all that, and then some.

MADONNA PAINTS A MUSTACHE & Other Close Encounters

"Elliott Gould said to Elvis Presley/'I may be crazy, but/ What's that gun doing/ Sitting on your hip?'"

"Mae West always made an entrance/Even when exiting."

After each of his celebrity encounters, Grobel wrote a short poem crystallizing his insights and impressions. Among the 150 people covered are Barbra Streisand, Goldie Hawn, Jake Gyllenhaal, Madonna, Saul Bellow, Bruce Springsteen, Farrah Fawcett, Nicole Kidman, Norman Mailer, Robert De Niro and Angelina Jolie.

ABOVE THE LINE: Conversations About the Movies

A dazzling gathering of insights and anecdotes from all corners of the film industry—interviews that reveal the skills, intelligence, experiences, and emotions of eleven key players who produce, write, direct, act in, and review the movies: Oliver Stone, Anthony Hopkins, Jodie Foster, Robert Evans, Lily Tomlin, Jean-Claude Van Damme, Harrison Ford, Robert Towne, Sharon Stone, and Siskel and Ebert. Joyce Carol Oates called *Above the Line*, "A diverse and lively collection, the highest art of the interview." Dylan McDermott wrote, "There are passages in this book that will leave you stunned."

ENDANGERED SPECIES: Writers Talk about Their Craft, Their Visions, Their Lives

Norman Mailer once told Lawrence Grobel that writers may be an endangered species. And Saul Bellow told him, "The country has changed so, that what I do no longer signifies anything, as it did when I was young." But to judge from this collection, writers and writing aren't done for quite yet. Twelve writers — Bellow, Mailer, Ray Bradbury, J.P. Donleavy, James Ellroy, Allen Ginsberg, Andrew Greeley, Alex Haley, Joseph Heller, Elmore Leonard, Joyce Carol Oates, and Neil Simon — memorably state their case for what they do and how they do it.

CLIMBING HIGHER

A *New York Times* Bestseller, *Climbing Higher* is the story of Montel Williams' life and personal struggles with multiple sclerosis. From initial denial through fear, depression, and anger, Williams emerged with a fierce determination not to be beaten down by MS. In addition, with the help of a team of leading doctors, *Climbing Higher* also offers information on new MS research and invaluable guidance for managing MS.

MARILYN & ME
In 1960 and 1962 Lawrence Schiller was asked by *Paris Match* and *Life* magazines to photograph Marilyn Monroe on the set of *Let's Make Love* and *Something's Got to Give*, which was never completed because of her controversial death. Schiller had befriended Monroe and he asked Lawrence Grobel to help him shape the story of that friendship into this memoir.

BARBRA STREISAND
This Taschen book reproduces the photographs of Streisand taken by Steve Schapiro and Lawrence Schiller over the years. Grobel has written the text, including interviews with both photographers.

Yoga? No! SHMOGA!
Google "Yoga" and 103,000,000 items come up. Yet for everyone who practices yoga, there are dozens of others who just sit and watch. *Yoga? No! Shmoga!* is for those who sit and watch, as well as for those who actually do yoga and have a sense of humor. Shmoga is the Lazy Man's Way to Inner Peace. In 43 short chapters it pokes fun at sports, religion, exercise, Wall Street, art, entertainment, and people looking for an excuse to not do anything more than lift a finger. It teaches you to take charge of your life, but in a clever way. Doing Shmoga actually makes sense!

Made in the USA
Middletown, DE
03 August 2021